‘No, *you* look, my sweet, head-strong, perverse wife.’

He had risen with one of the swift animal-like movements characteristic of him, and before she could react he had drawn her to her feet with both hands gripping her elbows as he held her in front of him. ‘I intend to talk this through.’

‘I don’t want to talk,’ she protested, angry at the way his nearness was affecting her equilibrium. ‘There’s nothing to say and no need to talk.’

‘Maybe you’re right at that.’ His eyes had locked on hers, drawing her into the glowing amber as he filled her vision. ‘Action speaks louder than words—isn’t that what they say?’

Helen Brooks lives in Northamptonshire and is married with three children. As she is a committed Christian, busy housewife and mother, her spare time is at a premium, but her hobbies include reading, swimming, gardening and walking her two energetic, inquisitive and very endearing young dogs. Her long-cherished aspiration to write became a reality when she put pen to paper on reaching the age of forty, and sent the result off to Mills & Boon.

Recent titles by the same author:
Modern Romance™

MISTRESS BY AGREEMENT
THE CHRISTMAS MARRIAGE MISSION

THE PASSIONATE HUSBAND

BY

HELEN BROOKS

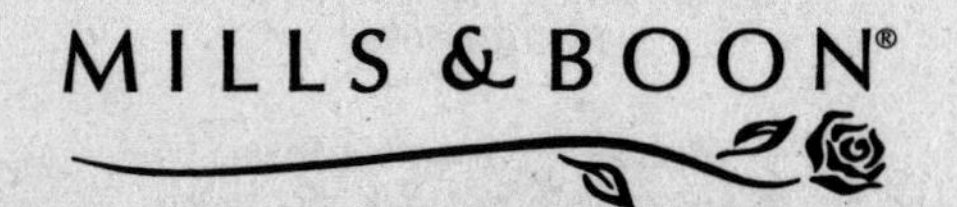

First published in Great Britain 2004
Harlequin Mills & Boon Limited,
Eton House, 18-24 Paradise Road, Richmond, Surrey TW9 1SR

ISBN 0 263 83760 2

Set in Times Roman 10½ on 12 pt.
01-0804-50793

Printed and bound in Spain
by Litografia Rosés, S.A., Barcelona

CHAPTER ONE

'I BET YOU'RE the only woman in the room who hasn't noticed the hunk with she who must be obeyed. Right?'

'What?'

Marsha raised startled emerald-green eyes, and the small plump girl standing in front of her sighed resignedly. 'I knew it. The whole place is buzzing with curiosity and there's you—as serene and cool as always.'

'Nicki, you know better than anyone else I need the facts and figures for the Baxter slot at my fingertips for the meeting tomorrow,' Marsha said patiently, reaching for the glass of fizzy mineral water at her side and taking a sip. 'As my secretary—'

'I'm talking as your friend, not your secretary,' Nicki responded smartly. 'This is supposed to be a little get-together as a reward for the current ratings and all our hard work, and you're the only one not taking advantage of the free food and booze. Don't you *like* champagne, for goodness' sake?' She wrinkled her snub nose at the hapless mineral water.

'Not particularly,' Marsha answered truthfully. It was a vastly overrated beverage in her opinion. 'And I like to keep a clear head when I'm working.'

'Ah, but you shouldn't *be* working,' Nicki pointed out triumphantly. 'It's once in a blue moon that the powers-that-be acknowledge what a great team they've got below them. Can't you take a few minutes to enjoy the moment?'

Now it was Marsha who sighed. When Nicki dug her

heels in she could be formidable. This made her an excellent secretary in some respects, but, as there was a distinct mother hen quirk to her extrovert personality, it could also be irritating.

Nicki was only three years older than her, at thirty, but the other woman appeared positively matronly most of the time. She was also loyal, trustworthy, hard-working and discreet, and Marsha counted herself fortunate to have Nicki in her corner in the cut-and-thrust world of television, the sector in which she had decided to make her career.

She gave mental affirmation to this last thought now as she said, 'Okay, okay, you win. One glass of champagne to keep you happy won't hurt, I guess.'

'Great.' Nicki's round pretty face beamed as she surveyed the slim delicate woman sitting on a sofa in a quiet recess of the bustling room. 'I presume you are coming out of your hidey-hole to drink it?'

'Hardly a hidey-hole, Nicki,' Marsha said drily. The recess was in full view of at least half the room where the drink and nibbles get-together was being thrown, and she'd had every intention of being sociable for a while once she had finished working. Now, stifling a sigh, Marsha rose to her feet, smoothing a lock of silver-blonde hair away from her face as she followed Nicki into the throng of animated noisy folk whose conversation had risen and ebbed like the tide for the last hour or so.

'So, where's the hunk, then?' Marsha glanced round the crowded room as Nicki handed her a glass of sparkling champagne. 'Penelope can't have eaten him already.'

Penelope Pelham was a top executive at the television company they worked for, with a well-deserved reputation for ruthlessness in every sphere of her life. It was an accepted fact that one would consider appealing to Penelope's kindness and compassion in the same way as a great white shark's.

Gossip had it that Penelope ate men up and spat them out in the same way she did any employee unfortunate enough to fall foul of her temper, and no one doubted this was true.

Marsha had never had cause to cross swords with the beautiful flamboyant brunette since she had started working for the television company some twelve months before, but that didn't mean she wasn't as wary of the other woman as everyone else. Penelope was powerful and influential, and the force of her dominant personality was impressive.

'Janie says they've just disappeared into Penelope's office with strict instructions from the lady herself they're not to be disturbed. Mind you, for once I have to say I see eye to eye with Penelope. If I had got my claws into a man like that, I'd want to be alone with him every moment I could get.'

Nicki gave a ridiculously hammed-up leer and Marsha began to laugh. She took a sip of the effervescent drink and found it to be surprisingly good. The bigwigs had pulled out all the stops for once. Normally the odd work do like this consisted of cheap plonk and sandwiches curling round the edges.

'Come and get some food.' Nicki was on a roll now, and Marsha didn't object when she was pulled over to the loaded table at the far end of the room. Knowing they were all expected to attend this gathering at the end of the working day, she'd skipped lunch in an effort to get the Baxter story under her belt. Now, as she looked at the very nice spread, without a curling ham sandwich in sight, she found she was hungry. Ravenous, in fact.

'Ooh, I just love kebabs, don't you?' Nicki was busy stocking up her plate. 'And this flan is delicious. And just *look* at those desserts. Janie had a free hand so she ordered them from Finns.'

Janie was Penelope's secretary, and Nicki had made it her business to strike up a friendship with the other woman—when Janie had started working for the company six months before—on the premise that you could never have too many friends in high places. Marsha wasn't sure if she agreed with this somewhat machiavellian viewpoint, but it was undoubtedly useful to have a secretary with her finger on the pulse, albeit second-hand.

'I presume you've asked Janie for the dope on the hunk?' Marsha asked idly, filling her own plate as she spoke and then picking up her glass of champagne and making her way over to a couple of vacant seats.

'Uh-huh.' Nicki demolished two bulging pastry *hors d'oeuvres*, licking her lips and rolling her eyes in appreciation, before she added, 'She didn't know anything.'

Marsha nodded. If she was being honest she would have said she wasn't in the least bit curious about Penelope's new man-friend, but she didn't want to hurt Nicki's feelings. Her secretary had been happily married to her childhood sweetheart for the last eleven years, but that didn't stop Nicki being a romance addict who read every book and saw every film with even the tiniest bit of amorous intrigue in it.

Marsha knew she had greatly disappointed the other woman when she'd made it clear, a few weeks after starting work at the company, that she wasn't interested in the opposite sex. And, no, she'd hastily added when Nicki's expression had made it clear what she was thinking, she wasn't interested in the female sex either! She had made the decision to concentrate on her career and only her career some time ago, that was all.

A few months later, when the two women had become friends as well as work colleagues, Marsha had admitted her decision had something to do with a man—once bitten, twice shy—but hadn't elaborated further. It said a lot for Nicki's strength of will that she had never brought the subject up again, merely confining herself to the odd remark about some dishy man she or her husband knew who had recently become single again, or pointing out that *everyone* indulged in one or two blind dates in their lives. Marsha normally responded to such obvious wiles by ignoring them and changing the subject.

'How come,' Nicki said thoughtfully, 'you can eat like you do and not put on a pound of weight? It's not fair.'

'I did miss lunch.' It was said gently. Nicki ate the equivalent of a three-course meal every lunchtime, and there was always a bag of sweets in her desk drawer which was replaced daily, not to mention hot sausage rolls from the canteen mid-morning, and cakes or biscuits mid-afternoon.

Nicki grinned. 'I wish everyone was as tactful as you, but I do so *enjoy* my food. And then there's those evenings when the urge to pig out is just irresistible, and chocolate just sort of leaps up and waves its hands. Know what I mean?'

'Marsha has never particularly cared for chocolate. Now, coconut ice is something else. I've known her to eat a pound or so of that all to herself in one sitting.'

The deep voice behind them was relaxed and cool, but as Marsha's head shot round she saw the sculptured features of the tall man standing with Penelope could have been carved in granite. Admittedly the hard mouth curled at the edges with something which could have been described as a smile by those who did not know better. But Marsha did know better. And how. She fought for control, willing herself not to stutter and stammer as she said, 'Taylor. What a surprise.'

'Isn't it?' The startling tawny eyes with their thick black lashes were fixed on her shocked face. 'But a pleasant one…for me, that is.'

'You two are obviously already acquainted,' Penelope drawled sweetly, her smile not quite reaching the blue eyes set in a face which was faintly exotic and very lovely. Marsha noticed the way the other woman's hand had tightened on Taylor's arm in an instinctive predatory gesture which said volumes.

She drew in a long, body-straightening breath and squared her shoulders. So that was how it was. But she should have known, shouldn't she, with Taylor's reputation? 'We knew each other once, a long time ago,' she said clearly, her tone dismissive. 'Now, if you'll excuse me, I've some work to finish—'

'Once? Oh, come on, Marsha, you'll have these good folk believing we were ships that passed in the night instead of man and wife.'

Nicki's mouth had dropped open to the point where she looked comical, but no one was looking at her.

Marsha's clear green eyes widened infinitesimally, even as she told herself she should have expected this. Taylor being Taylor, he wouldn't let her get away with snubbing him. A vein in her temple throbbed, but her voice was quiet when she said, 'Goodbye, Taylor.'

'You were *married*?' In any other circumstances Marsha would have enjoyed seeing the ice-cool Penelope dumbfounded.

'Not were, Penelope. Are.' Taylor's voice was as quiet as Marsha's had been, but the steely note made it twice as compelling. 'Marsha is my wife.'

'Until the divorce is finalised.' She had turned, but now she swung back as she shot the words at him. 'And that would have happened a long time ago if I'd had my way.'

Her voice had risen slightly, calling forth one or two interested glances from people around them who hadn't heard what had been said but who recognised anger when they heard it.

'But...but your surname is Gosling, isn't it?'

Penelope was staring at her as though she'd never seen her before, and in spite of the awfulness of the moment there was an element of satisfaction in being able to reply, 'Gosling is my maiden name. Personnel are aware of my marital status—albeit temporary.' She flashed a scathing glance at the tall dark man at Penelope's side. 'But when I said I prefer to be known as Miss Gosling on a day-to-day basis they saw no reason to object.'

'This is most irregular.' Penelope had recovered her composure and her tone was frosty. 'I should have been informed.'

Marsha could have said here that her immediate boss, Jeff North, was fully aware of her circumstances, but she wasn't about to get into a discussion on the rights and wrongs of it all with Penelope. Not with Taylor standing there with his eyes fixed on her face.

The brief glances she'd bestowed on him had told her he was as devastatingly attractive as ever. He had never been textbook handsome, his appeal was too virile and manly for that, but the hard, rugged features offset by tawny cat eyes and jet-black hair radiated magnetism. And the strong, tough face was set above a body which was just as vigorous, its sinewy muscles and a powerful frame ensuring women everywhere gave him a second glance. Or three or four or more.

This last thought made Marsha's voice every bit as cold as Penelope's when she said, 'Possibly. Now, if you'll excuse me?' And she left without a backward glance.

It wasn't until she got in the lift and attempted to press the button for the third floor that Marsha realised how much her hands were shaking. She stood stiff and straight until the doors had glided to, and then leant limply against the carpeted side of the lift, her stomach swirling. Taylor—here. What was she going to do?

And then the answer came, as though from somewhere outside herself. Nothing. You are going to do nothing, because nothing has changed from how things were this morning. He is not in your life any more. He can't hurt you.

But if that was true why was she feeling as though her whole world had collapsed around her right now? The world she had carefully built up over the last months?

Shock. The answer was there again. Shock, pure and simple. It was so unexpected, seeing him like that. You were unprepared, taken off guard. But that doesn't mean you aren't over him.

The lift had stopped, and now the doors opened again, but for a moment Marsha stood staring blankly ahead, her mind racing. She wasn't over him. She'd never be over him. You didn't get over someone like

Taylor. You just learnt to live with the pain that it was over.

'Enough.' She spoke out loud, the courage and self-respect which had enabled her to leave him in the first place coming to her aid. 'No snivelling, no crying. You've cried enough tears to fill an ocean as it is.'

Once in the office she shared with Nicki, Jeff North's room being separated from theirs by an interjoining door, Marsha sat down at her desk with a little plump. Of all the places in all the world, why was Taylor here? And *was* he Penelope's new lover? The thought brought such a shaft of pain she pushed it to the back of her consciousness to think about later, once she was home. For now she had to get out of this place with a semblance of dignity, and she'd do it if it killed her.

It was at that point she realised she'd left her handbag, along with the papers she'd been looking at when Nicki had pounced on her, downstairs in the alcove. She muttered something very rude before leaning back in the seat and shutting her eyes for a moment. Great, just great. She'd have to go and retrieve everything, which would totally ruin the decorous exit she'd just made.

Footsteps brought her eyes snapping open and her back straightening, but it was Nicki who emerged in the doorway, and she was clutching the Baxter file and Marsha's handbag. 'You forgot these,' she said awkwardly. 'Are you all right?'

'Sort of.' Marsha managed a weak smile. 'Thanks for these.'

'All in a day's work.'

Marsha had expected a barrage of questions the next time she saw Nicki, but when the other girl sat down at her own desk and began packing her things away, all she said was, 'They've gone, by the way, Penelope and your—and him.'

'Right.' She'd explain a little tomorrow, but tonight she couldn't face it. 'I'm off too. We'll talk in the morning, Nicki,' she said, rising to her feet and reaching for her jacket. It was her brisk boss tone, something Marsha used rarely, but when she did Nicki knew enough to take the hint.

Once she was in the lift again, a thousand butterflies began to do an Irish jig in Marsha's stomach. What if Nicki was wrong and he was waiting for her in Reception? She wouldn't put it past Taylor. She wouldn't put *anything* past Taylor Kane.

Reception was the usual madhouse at this time of night, but it was Taylorless and that was all Marsha asked. She responded to a couple of goodnights, raising a hand in farewell to Bob, the security guard, with whom she often had a chat when she was working late and it was quieter. He regaled her with tales of his six children, who had all gone off the rails in some way or other and who drove Bob and his long-suffering wife mad, but tonight Marsha felt she would swap places with them like a shot.

Once outside, in the warm June evening, Marsha looked about her, only relaxing and breathing more easily after a few moments of scanning the bustling crowd. Everyone was walking fast and every other person was talking into a mobile phone. Irate drivers were honking car horns, there was the occasional screech of tyres and the odd person or so was dicing with death by ignoring pedestrian crossings and throwing themselves in front of the rush hour traffic. A normal evening, in fact.

It was too warm for the jacket she'd worn that morning, and now she tucked it over her arm as she began to walk past Notting Hill towards Kensington. Somehow she couldn't face the jam-packed anonymity of the tube or a bus tonight. It would take a while to get to her tiny bedsit deep in West Kensington, but the walk through Holland Park was pleasant on an evening like this, and she needed some time to collect her whirling thoughts and sort out her emotions. And then she wrinkled her small straight nose at the thought. Since when had she ever been able to get her head round her feelings for Taylor?

'I had a feeling you'd walk.'

Her pulse leapt as the deep voice at her elbow registered, and in that moment she knew she had been expecting him to make an appearance. She didn't turn her head, and she was pleased her voice was so cool—considering her racing heartbeat—when she said, 'Clever you.'

'How are you, Fuzz?'

His pet name for her caused her traitorous heart to lurch before she quelled the weakness. Fuzz had come into being on their second date, when he had said he thought goslings were supposed to be all fluff and down, his eyes on her sleek shiny hair. She'd smiled, answering that fuzz and feathers weren't compulsory, and from that moment—whenever they were alone—he'd whispered the name in a smoky tone which had caused her knees to buckle. But that was then and this was now. Her voice tight, she said, 'Don't call me that.'

'Why? You used to like it.'

His arrogance provoked her into raising angry eyes to meet his gaze, and she knew immediately it was a mistake. He was too close, for one thing. She could see the furrows in the tanned skin of his face, the laughter lines which crinkled the corners of his eyes. She caught her breath, steadying herself before she said, 'I'm glad you used the past tense.'

He shrugged, a casual easy movement she envied. 'Past, present, future—it's all the same. You're mine, Fuzz. You've been mine from the first moment we met.'

For a moment the urge to strike out in action as well as words was so strong it shocked her, but it acted like a bucket of cold water on her hot fury. Men like him never changed, she knew that, so why had she expected any different? Everything about Taylor whispered wealth and power and limitless control. She had married him knowing he was dangerous, but she had hoped she'd captured his heart. She had been wrong. 'I don't think so, Taylor. We'll be divorced soon, and that is the end of the road.'

'You think a piece of paper makes any difference one way or the other?' He took her arm, pulling her to a stop as he encircled her with his arms. 'This nonsense has to stop. Do you understand? I've been patient long enough.'

His height and breadth dwarfed her slender shape, and the familiar smell of him—a subtle mixture of deliciously sexy aftershave, clean male skin and something that was peculiarly Taylor—sent her senses reeling. *Control, control, control.* He was a past master of it—she had learnt it day by painful day in the months they had been separated. She couldn't let all that agony be for nothing. She ignored the longing which made her want to melt against the hard wall of his chest, saying instead, her voice clipped, 'Let go of me or I'll scream my head off. I mean it.'

'Scream away,' he offered lazily, but she had seen the narrowing of his eyes and the tightening of his mouth and she knew she had scored a hit.

She remained absolutely rigid and still in his arms, her eyes blazing, and after another long moment he let her go. 'You're still not prepared to listen to reason?'

'Reason?' She forced a scornful laugh, taking a step backwards and treading on some poor man's toe with her wafer-thin heels. His muffled yelp went unheeded.

'Yes, reason. Reason, logic, common sense—all those worthy attributes which seem to be so sadly lacking within that beautiful frame of yours,' he drawled, deliberately provocative.

Marsha gritted her teeth for a moment. He was the one person in all the world who could make her madder than hell in two seconds flat. 'Your definition of reason and logic is different from mine,' she said scathingly. 'I go by the *Oxford Dictionary*.'

'Meaning?'

'Meaning I don't hold with your clarification that reason means a promiscuous lifestyle where anything goes, and logic says you only begin to worry if you are caught out.'

He surveyed her defiant face expressionlessly, the magnificent tawny eyes glittering in the tanned darkness of his face. After an eternity, and very softly, he said, 'I see.'

Marsha stared back at him, determined not to let him see the quiet response had taken the wind out of her sails. She had been married to this man for three years, eighteen months of which she had been separated from him, but she'd had no idea how he would react to what she had said. Which summed up their relationship, really, she thought wretchedly. And was one of the reasons why she had left him and would never go back. *That and the other women.*

Her small chin rose a fraction, and now her voice had

lost its heat and was icy when she said, 'Good. It will save me having to repeat myself.'

'You look wonderful.' It was as though her previous words had never been voiced. 'Businesslike…' His gaze roamed over her curves, neatly ensconced in a jade-green pencil-slim skirt and a blouse of a slightly lighter hue. 'But still good enough to eat,' he added as his eyes returned to hers once more.

Marsha ignored the way her body had responded to the hunger in his face and concentrated on maintaining her equanimity. 'Don't try the Kane charm on me, Taylor,' she said coolly. 'I'm immune now.'

'Is that so?' His hand came up to tuck a strand of her hair behind her ear, his fingers lingering for a moment at her neck and setting off a chain reaction she knew he could sense. 'I don't think so.'

She hated him: his arrogance, his supreme confidence in his mastery over her mind, soul and body… She caught the bitterness, forcing it down where the astute amber eyes couldn't see and taking a deep hidden breath before she said, 'Then you must believe what you like. It really doesn't matter any more. In a month or so we will be divorced and free agents, and—'

'The hell we will.'

She ignored the interruption and hoped she hadn't revealed her composure was only skin-deep. 'And we can put the past behind us,' she finished evenly.

'You really think I will just let you walk away from me for ever?' He raised dark brows. 'You know me better than that.'

'I have never known you.' She had answered too quickly, her voice raw for a moment, and immediately she knew her mistake. She had to be calm and collected in front of him; it was her best defence. 'Just as you never really knew me,' she added quickly. 'We both thought each other was someone different. That was our mistake.'

'*Our* mistake?' The dark brows rose even higher. 'Did I hear correctly? You're actually admitting you're capable of being wrong occasionally?'

She would have given the world to sock him right on the jaw. Her neck and shoulders were stiff with the effort it was taking to remain poised and dignified, but she conquered the desire to wipe the slight smile off his face, although not without some gritting of teeth. When she could trust herself to speak, she said sweetly, 'I've nothing more to say to you. Goodbye, Taylor,' turning on her heel as she spoke his name.

It was only a moment or two before she realised he was walking alongside her. 'What are you doing?' she asked frostily.

'Walking you back home.' He didn't actually add, Of course, but he might as well have.

'I don't want you to.'

'Okay.' He stopped, but as she walked on, head high and heart thumping a tattoo, he called, 'I'll pick you up at eight, so be ready.'

'What?' She whirled round, causing a middle-aged woman with a huge bag of shopping to bump into her. When she had finished apologising she marched over to where Taylor was standing, arms crossed, as he leant against a convenient lamppost. 'Are you mad?' she asked in a tight voice.

'Me?' The innocence was galling. 'It was you who nearly knocked that poor woman off her feet.'

'You know what I mean.' She glared at him, wondering how she could have forgotten quite how attractive he was. There were very few men with truly black hair, but Taylor was one of them, and the contrast between his eyes and hair had always been riveting. Brushing this traitorous thought aside, she continued, 'I have no intention of having dinner with you, Taylor. Not today, not tomorrow, not ever. We're getting a *divorce*, for goodness' sake.'

He smiled. Marsha caught her breath. His smile had always affected her, like warm sunshine flooding over a stormy sea, possibly because he did it so rarely. Not genuine smiles anyway. 'Then what are you so afraid of?' he asked silkily. 'I'm merely suggesting we have dinner together, not that we finish the evening in bed.'

Her pulse jumped and then raced frantically as her body remembered what it had been like to be in bed with this man. To be loved, utterly and completely. To be consumed by him until all rational thought was gone and all that existed was Taylor. But then it hadn't been love, had it? At least not as she interpreted the word. Love and marriage meant commitment, faithfulness and loyalty as far as she was concerned, and she was blowed if she was going to apologise for feeling that way. 'I'm not afraid,' she said shakily. 'Don't be so ridiculous.'

'Then have dinner with me. For the time being at least we are still man and wife, Fuzz. Can't we try to be civilised?' His eyes were searching hers in that old way she remembered from when they had still been together. He had always looked at her like this in moments of stress or importance, as though he was trying to see the inner core of her, the essence of what made her *her*.

Marsha blinked, breaking the spell the glowing tawny colour that circled fierce black centres had wrought. She clutched at a reason for refusal. 'What about Penelope?' she said. 'Won't she mind?'

'Penelope?' He repeated the name as though he didn't have the faintest idea who the woman was, and then he said softly, 'Penelope Pelham is a business colleague, that's all. I'm quoting for new sound equipment and a load of stuff and she is my contact.'

Oh, yes? Who was kidding who? It had been as plain as the nose on her face that Penelope had decided Taylor was her next bedfellow. Kane International might well be putting in a tender for the new equipment they had all heard was being acquired, but if Taylor's firm won the work it would be because he had provided proof that his equipment was the best in more ways than one. Marsha blinked again. That last thought was not like her—but that was Taylor all over, she thought irritably. Bringing out the worst in her. 'I don't think dinner is a good idea,' she said firmly.

'It's an excellent idea,' he said, even more firmly.

'I'm trying to say no nicely.' She eyed him severely.

'Try saying yes badly.'

He was so close his warm breath fanned the silk of her hair, and for a moment she wanted to breathe in the smell and feel of him in great gulps. Instead the intensity of her emotion acted like a shot of adrenalin. 'It might surprise you, Taylor Kane, but you can't always have what you want,' she said steadily, the blood surging through her veins in a tumult.

'Not always, no.' This time he didn't smile. 'But tonight is not one of those times. Eight on the dot. I'm quite prepared to break the door down if you play coy.'

She was so surprised when he upped and walked away that for a good thirty seconds she was speechless. Then she called after him, oblivious of the passers-by, 'You don't know where I live!'

He turned just long enough to say, 'I have always known where you are, every minute since you've been gone.' And after that she found she was unable to say another word.

CHAPTER TWO

WHEN Marsha opened the front door of her bedsit a little while later, it was with the disturbing realisation that she couldn't remember a moment of the walk home. Her head had been so full of Taylor and their conversation, not least his ridiculous presumption that she would eat dinner with him, that the stroll she normally so enjoyed at the end of the working day had been accomplished on automatic.

Her bedsit was on the top floor of a three-storey terraced house, and in the last twelve months since she had been living in it Marsha had made it her own haven, away from the stress and excitement of her working life. She stood on the threshold for a moment, glancing round the sun-filled room in front of her, and as always a sense of pleasure made itself felt.

The room had been a mess when she had first viewed it, the previous occupiers having been a pair of young female students who clearly had never been introduced to soap and water or cleaning materials in the whole of their lives. She had scrubbed and scoured and cleaned for days, but eventually, after plenty of elbow grease and some deep thought on what she wanted, she had begun to decorate.

First she had stripped the old floorboards, which had been in surprisingly good condition, and once they were finished, she'd known how to proceed. She had painted the whole bedsit in a palette of gentle shades of off-white and cream, which harmonised with each other and the different tones of wood in the floorboards, before splashing out on organdie curtains for the two wide floor-to-ceiling windows, along with ecru blinds which she only pulled at night when it was dark and she was getting ready for bed.

The small sitting and sleeping area was separated from the kitchen by a sleek and beautiful glass breakfast bar, which Mrs Tate-Collins—Marsha's elderly landlady, who lived in the basement along with her three cats—had had installed in each of the three bedsits when she'd had the house converted after her husband had died. The *pièce de résistance* for Marsha, however, and the thing which had really sold the bedsit to her when she had first viewed it, was Mrs Tate-Collins's forethought in providing a tiny shower room in a recess off the kitchen. It was only large enough to hold a shower, loo and small corner washbasin, but all the other bedsits she had viewed at the time had necessitated a walk along a landing to a communal bathroom.

Once she had bought a sofabed, TV and two wooden stools for the breakfast bar, which served as her dining table, Marsha had left the bed and breakfast she had lived in since her split with Taylor and moved into her new home, adding touches like the ecru throw and tumbled cushions of soft ash-gold, stone and cream for the sofa as she had lived there.

The slim built-in wardrobe to one side of the front door, which held all her clothes, meant she had to be selective in what she bought, and the kitchen was only large enough to house the smallest of fridges, along with the built-in hob and oven, but Marsha didn't mind the lack of space. The bedsit was her retreat, somewhere she could shut the rest of the world out whenever she wanted to.

Her miniature garden was in the form of a Juliet balcony opening out from the windows, and although it could only hold one small wicker chair, along with a profusion of scented plants, she spent a good deal of her free time there in the warmer months, reading, dozing and looking out over the rooftops.

She loved her home. Marsha walked across to the windows now, opening them wide and letting the scents from the small balcony drift into the room. And now Taylor was going to come here, and that would spoil everything. She did not want him in her hideaway. She didn't want him in her *life*.

The hum of evening traffic from the busy main street beyond the cul-de-sac the house was situated in was louder now the windows were open. Normally Marsha didn't even hear the sound, so used had she become to the background noise. Tonight, though, it registered on her consciousness, and she found herself wondering what Taylor would make of the bedsit. The downstairs cloakroom in his lovely home deep in Harrow was about the same size as her entire living space.

'I don't care what he thinks.' She spoke out loud, flexing her shoulders as though to dislodge a weight there. 'And there is absolutely no way I am going out to dinner with him.'

So saying, she roused herself and walked into the kitchen, fixing herself a mug of milky chocolate which she took out on to the balcony. She sat down with a sigh, curling up on the big soft cushion in the wicker chair as she gazed out into space, a frown between her eyes.

Thirty minutes later and she had had a shower, and her hair was bundled under a soft handtowel as she stood surveying her meagre wardrobe.

She was only going to dinner with him to prevent a scene, she assured herself silently. A scene which would undoubtedly occur if Taylor did not get his own way. But this was strictly a one-off, something she would make perfectly clear to him, as well as letting him know she was counting the days until the divorce when all ties would be cut for good.

She pulled a pair of slinky, slightly flared pants in a misty silver colour from the wardrobe, teaming them with a bolero-style silk jacket in pale green. They were the newest items of clothing she possessed, bought for a cocktail party she had attended a month or so before. After placing the clothes on the back of the sofa she walked over to the full-length mirror on the back of the wardrobe door, staring at herself long and hard for a moment or two.

How could Taylor imagine, even for one single second, that there was any hope for them after what he had done? But then she *had* walked away from Taylor, rather than it being the other way round, something he would have found insupportable. To her knowledge, no woman had ever ended a relationship with him before—it had always been Taylor who had ditched them. Which was probably why his ego had been big enough to think he could have his cake and eat it.

This last reflection brought Marsha's lips into a thin line as she pictured the 'cake' in question. Tanya West—a voluptuous redhead with the body of Marilyn Monroe and the face of an angel. And according to Susan, Taylor's sister, Tanya hadn't been the first little dalliance he'd indulged in since his marriage.

She whipped the towel off her head, beginning to blow dry her hair into a soft silky bob and all the time denying the hurt and anger which had flared up at the thought of the other woman.

She was still denying it when the buzzer next to the door sounded forty minutes later. Pressing the little switch, she stared at Taylor's face—small and very far away—as she said, 'I'll be down in just a second.' She didn't open the front door of the building, deciding he could think what he liked.

One last swift glance in the mirror told her she was looking cool and controlled, despite the way her heart was pounding, and she offered up a quick prayer that the illusion would hold during the time she was with Taylor. He had to understand she wasn't the same gullible fool who had been so besotted with him she hadn't seen what was in front of her nose. She had thought he'd accepted that when she had left him and refused to see him eighteen months ago, especially in view of the fact there had been no objection from his solicitor—to her knowledge—when she had filed for divorce.

Locking the door of the bedsit behind her, she made for the stairs, careful how she descended in the high strappy sandals she was wearing, and it was as she approached the ground floor that she heard the unmistakable sound of Taylor's voice talking to someone inside the house. Someone had let him into the hall. She froze for a moment on the stairs, her ears straining to hear whom he was speaking to.

Mrs Tate-Collins. As Marsha identified the other voice she raised her eyes heavenwards. Her landlady was a sweetie-pie, but the elderly lady really belonged in a powder and crinoline age, where men were gallant and noble and all women were prone to attacks of the vapours. Mrs Tate-Collins had told her once of her privileged upbringing and her private education at home and then an establishment for well brought up young gentlewomen. When Marsha had said she had been raised in a children's home after her single-parent mother had abandoned her when she was two years old the other woman had stared at her as though she was a creature from another planet. Not that she hadn't been sympathetic, Marsha qualified, but it had been plain the other woman was out of her depth with such an alien concept. How Mrs Tate-Collins was going to cope with finding out Miss Gosling was really Mrs Kane, Marsha didn't know.

'Ah, here she is, Mr Kane,' Mrs Tate-Collins trilled as Marsha came into view. 'And looking very lovely.'

Marsha gave what she hoped was a neutral smile. 'Thank you,' she said directly to the other woman, before glancing at Taylor, whereupon the smile iced over. 'I told you I'd be straight down,' she said evenly. 'There was no need to come in.'

'Oh, I was just on my way across the hall after seeing Miss Gordon when your young man rang,' Mrs Tate-Collins chimed in before Taylor could speak, turning to him as she added, 'That's the lady who lives on this floor, you know, the poor thing. She had a fall the other day and it has shaken her up a little, so I took her a drop of soup and a roll to save her having to think about supper. She is getting on a bit, bless her.'

Marsha saw Taylor gaze into the lined face of the small wizened woman in front of him, who looked ninety if a day, but his voice was perfectly serious when he said, 'That was kind of you, Mrs Tate-Collins.'

'Shall we go?' It was clear Taylor hadn't got round to mentioning their marital status, which suited her just fine, and she was anxious to get him out of the door before her landlady started another cosy chat. 'Goodbye, Mrs Tate-Collins,' she added briskly.

'Oh, goodbye, dear.'

It was a little surprised, but in view of the fact Marsha had gripped Taylor's arm with one hand and opened the front door with the other, virtually pushing him on to the top step, she really couldn't blame her landlady.

'She'll think you can't wait to have your wicked way with me.' Once they had descended the eight steps and were on the pavement Taylor raised an amused eyebrow at her.

Up to this moment she had successfully fought acknowledging how drop-dead gorgeous he looked, but as her heart missed a couple of beats she said stiffly, 'Mrs Tate-Collins would never think anything so vulgar.'

'Really? I thought she had a little twinkle in her eye.'

Any female, whatever her age, would have a twinkle in her eye when she looked at Taylor. That was the effect he had on the whole of womankind. 'I think not,' she said crisply. 'And before we move from here I want to make it perfectly plain that I have agreed to this meeting under sufferance, and only because I want the divorce to go through with the minimum of disruption.'

Taylor surveyed her silently, his customary stern expression now in place. 'Feel better now you've got that off your chest?' he asked mildly after a very long moment.

Marsha shrugged. 'I just wanted you to know, that's all,' she said, wondering why she suddenly felt like a recalcitrant schoolgirl.

'Believe me, Fuzz, I was never in any doubt,' he said drily. 'You are nothing if not straightforward.'

Which was more than could be said for him.

She hadn't spoken, but the words must have been

plain to read on her face because he next said, even more drily, 'Especially when you say nothing at all.'

'So, in view of that, why are we doing this?' she asked a touch bewilderedly. He hadn't contacted her in almost eighteen months, so why now, with the divorce just weeks away?

'Because it's time.'

He had always been good at those—the cryptic one-liners. Right from when she had first met him she had known he was an enigma, but she had thought she'd found the key when he'd asked her to marry him just weeks after they had first been introduced at a dinner party by a mutual friend. Love. She had mistakenly imagined he loved her as she loved him—*had* loved him, she corrected immediately. *Had.*

The warm evening was redolent with the faint smells of cooking from various open windows, along with the strains of a popular chart hit and bursts of laughter from the house next door. Marsha watched Taylor wrinkle his aquiline nose. 'Shall we go?' he asked quietly, his eyes tight on her face.

She would have liked to have said no and turned on her heel, but it really wasn't an option. She nodded, allowing him to take her arm as they walked a few steps to where his Aston Martin was parked. He had changed the model in the last eighteen months, she noted silently, although the other car had only been six months old when she had left him. This one was sleek and dark and dangerous—very much like Taylor.

He opened the passenger door for her, and she slid into the expensive interior with a gracefulness she was pleased about, considering the way her stomach was jumping and her legs were trembling. That was the trouble with Taylor, she thought irritably. However much she tried to prepare herself, he always got under her skin.

Once he had joined her in the car, she steeled herself to glance at him as though his closeness bothered her not at all. 'Where are we going?'

'Surprise.' He didn't look at her, starting the engine and then manoeuvring the powerful car out of the close confines of the parking space. Her eyes fell on the thick gold ring on the third finger of his left hand, and again her heart lurched. Did he wear his wedding band all the time, or had he donned it specially for this evening? she asked herself, before answering in the next breath, what did it matter anyway? The ring was just an item of jewellery if the commitment it was meant to signify wasn't there. Her own hands had been ringless from the moment she had walked out of their house and out of Taylor's life.

The car purred along the busy London streets, passing numerous pubs and wine bars where folk were sitting outside drinking or eating in the dying sunshine. In the interim between leaving university and meeting Taylor Marsha had often enjoyed summer evenings with friends in this way, but since the breakdown of her marriage she hadn't wanted to go back to the old crowd. She still saw one or two of them occasionally, but it wasn't the same—not for her. They were still all relatively fancy-free and into having a good time, but she felt she had passed that stage and couldn't go back—certainly not while she was still legally a married woman anyway. Stupid, maybe, she admitted a trifle bitterly, considering the way Taylor had behaved, but she couldn't help it.

She glanced down at her hands, which were tight fists in her lap, and forced her fingers to relax, uncurling them one by one as she breathed deeply and willed her pulse into a steady beat. 'I don't like surprises,' she said clearly, as though Taylor had just spoken that moment rather than all of ten minutes ago. Ten minutes of ragged vibrating silence.

She kept her gaze on the windscreen as the tawny eyes flashed over her tight profile before returning to the road ahead. 'Shame,' he drawled smoothly.

'So, where are we going?' And then, as the car made another turning, she knew. He was taking her home! No, not home—home was now her tiny sanctuary in West Kensington. 'Stop the car please, Taylor,' she said as evenly as she could.

'Why?'

His tone was so innocent she knew she was right. 'Because you told me you were taking me out to dinner,' she said stonily.

'I am.' He gestured with one hand at the immaculate dinner suit he was wearing.

'Taylor!' She paused, warning herself to take care not to lose her temper and give him the satisfaction of winning. 'I recognise where we are,' she said more calmly. 'This is a stone's throw from Harrow.'

He nodded, totally unrepentant. 'That's right, and Hannah has been like a dog with two tails knowing you were dropping by tonight.'

Dropping by? Was the man mad? And then the thought of the buxom, middle-aged housekeeper who had mothered her from the first moment she had been introduced to her melted Marsha enough for a lump to come into her throat. She bit down on the emotion, saying, 'I have no intention of going to your home.'

'Our home, Fuzz.' His voice was suddenly dangerous. 'And although you might be able to cast people off as though they have never existed, Hannah can't. Mad as you were with me, it wouldn't have hurt you to have dropped her a line or arranged to meet her somewhere. Even a phone call would have been something. You damn near broke her heart.'

She couldn't stand this. Didn't he know that any reminder of him, however small, had crucified her in the early days, and if she had seen Hannah all her resolve to be strong and make a new life would have been swept away? She had missed the woman who had become the only mother she had ever known nearly as much as Taylor. And then, because she was working on sheer emotion, and without the necessary protective shields in place, she spoke out the thing which had hurt her as much as his betrayal with Tanya. 'If you were so concerned about Hannah's feelings, why didn't you contact me after I'd left?' she bit out harshly. 'You're a fine one to talk about casting people off.'

'I don't believe I'm hearing this,' he growled, raking back his hair with an angry gesture which spoke volumes. 'I came home after three days in Germany which had been pure hell to find you already packed and waiting to leave. You came at me all guns firing and accusing me of goodness knows what, and when I tried to make you see reason you walked out of the door. I followed you to your car to prevent you leaving and you slammed the door on my hand, breaking several bones in the process.'

'That was an accident,' she defended quickly. 'I said so at the time, if you remember. I didn't know you'd got your hand in the way of the door.'

'It didn't prevent you from driving off though, did it?' he reminded her heatedly.

Marsha took a moment to compose herself. He was

turning this all round, as though she was the one who had had an affair! 'Hannah was there to take care of you—'

'Damn Hannah,' he said furiously, as though he hadn't just accused her of being unfeeling. 'I drove after you, if you remember, and do you recall what you said when we stopped at those traffic lights? If I didn't stop following you, you'd drive into a wall. Tell me you didn't mean that.'

She had meant it. She had been so desperate and hurt that night it would have been a relief not to have to think or feel ever again.

He nodded grimly. 'Quite,' he said, as though she had just confirmed what he'd said out loud. 'So I let you go. Call me old-fashioned, but I thought I'd rather see you alive than dead.'

'Call *me* old-fashioned, but I always thought there were two in a marriage, not three—or more.'

She saw a muscle in his cheek twitch at her direct hit, but his voice was suddenly much calmer when he said, 'Tanya again.'

She ignored that, continuing, 'And my point still remains the same. You did not contact me after that night.'

'Not physically, maybe, but surely the letter counts for something?'

'Letter?' She hadn't received a letter and she didn't believe for one moment he had written one. Whatever game he was playing, she wasn't going to fall for it.

'Oh, come on, Fuzz,' he said wearily. 'Don't pretend you didn't receive my letter.'

His tone brought her temper to boiling point once more. 'I *never* pretend,' she said hotly, 'and I don't lie either. I did not receive a letter, although if I had it would have made no difference whatsoever to how I felt—feel. You had an affair with Tanya West and there had been others before her. I have that on good authority. You shared a double room in Germany reserved under the name of Mr and Mrs Kane. Don't lie to me about that because I phoned the hotel myself to check.'

'Tanya was my secretary and only my secretary,' he ground out, swinging the car round a sharp corner at such speed Marsha had to stifle a little scream. 'The room in Germany was booked in error. She had the double and I took the only other bed in the whole damn place, due to the conference, and spent three nights sharing a twin with a huge Swede who looked as though he weight-lifted for his country and snored like hell. I told you that on the night you left and reiterated it in the letter.'

'Then why was I put through to Tanya when I asked for Mr Kane after the receptionist had confirmed the double room?' Marsha asked as icily as her raw nerves would allow. The way he was driving they would be lucky to see another day.

'I've told you, the room was booked in error. The Swede kindly allowed me to share his room when the hotel asked him, but the room was in his name, not mine. Maybe the receptionist you spoke to hadn't been informed of what had happened. It was one of the biggest conferences of the year, damn it, and the place was heaving.'

He must think she was born yesterday.

'You don't believe me.' As he accelerated to pass a staid family saloon she sat tensely silent because there was nothing more to say. 'I gave you telephone numbers to ring in that letter, and not just the hotel. I had the Swede's business card. I also made you a promise, because of the way you had reacted that night in the car, that I wouldn't try to force you to see me until you were ready, and being ready meant an apology and a declaration of trust.'

The *nerve* of him. Even if all this with Tanya was a mistake—and she didn't think it was for a moment—what about the other liaisons Susan had told her about? Taylor bought silence from people, but he hadn't been able to buy Susan's. Susan had been her friend as well as her sister-in-law, and the episode in Germany had been too much for the other woman to ignore. Susan had sworn her to secrecy at the time, making her promise she wouldn't tell who it was who had informed on him—mainly because Susan's husband worked for her brother and their livelihood depended on Taylor's favour. Well, she hadn't betrayed Susan eighteen months ago and she wasn't about to do so now, much as she would have loved to fling his sister's name into the arena.

She took a deep pull of air. 'If the letter said you wouldn't contact me until I was ready to apologise and trust you, why are we here now? I don't trust you, Taylor, and I would rather walk through coals of fire than apologise to you.'

He muttered something under his breath before saying, his voice curt, 'I am not going to allow you to wreck both our lives, that's why. Not through foolish pride.'

Pride? If they hadn't been travelling at such speed she would have been tempted to knock his block off, she thought poetically. As it was she contented herself with saying scathingly, 'I've salvaged by life and it's a good one, so speak for yourself.'

'I don't believe you.'

They were now in territory she recognised as being a street or so away from where Taylor's palatial home dwelt, so in view of her safety, and everyone else's within the immediate vicinity, she waited until the car had actually passed through the open gates and was travelling up the scrunchy drive before she said, 'That's your problem.'

He brought the car to a standstill at the bottom of the wide, semi-circular stone steps which led up to the front door, and Marsha forced herself to look about her as though her heart didn't feel as though it was being torn out by its roots. She had been almost demented with bitterness and pain when she had last left here, and certainly in no state to drive. She had hoped if she ever saw this place again she would be able to look at it with a measure of peace in her heart, but it wasn't the case. She felt nearly as wretched with misery as she had then.

Taylor hadn't answered her before he slid out of the car and walked round the bonnet to open her door, and now, as she took the hand he proferred and exited the Aston Martin, the haunting fragrance of lavender teased her nostrils. A bowling-green-smooth lawn bordered both sides of the curving drive, and the huge thatched house was framed by two cooper beech trees, their leaves glowing in the last of the sunlight, but it was the tiny hedges of lavender which ran from the bottom of the largest step in a wide half-moon shape right up to the corners of the house which produced the most evocative memory.

It had been this perfume which had remained with her the first time she had ever visited the house, on her second date with Taylor, and which had scented their nights in their big billowy bed when they had made love till dawn with the windows open to the scents and sounds of the night.

The pain which gripped her now wasn't helped by the warm contact with his skin, which sent a hundred tiny needles of sensation shivering up her arm, and as soon as she was standing she extricated her hand from his.

'You loved this place when the lavender was out.' Taylor spoke quietly, his eyes tight on her pale face.

Her green eyes shot to meet hot amber. He had waited and planned to bring her here when the conditions were just right for maximum effect. She could read it in his face even if his words hadn't confirmed it. The words she hissed at him would have shocked the motherly Hannah into a coma.

Taylor surveyed her flushed face thoughtfully. 'Are you sure that last suggestion is anatomically possible?'

She glared at him. 'You are the most manipulative, scheming, cunning man I've ever met.'

A corner of his mouth twitched. 'Thank you. I think you're pretty exceptional too.'

Suddenly the anger and resentment left her body in a great whoosh of sadness and regret for what might have been if he had been different. Or maybe if *she* had been different? If she had been bright and beautiful and sophisticated, like the women he had dated before he'd met her, maybe then he would have continued to love her and wouldn't have needed anyone else. Maybe then she would have been enough for him?

She wasn't aware of the expression on her face, or the droop to her mouth, so when he said, very softly, 'I want you back, Fuzz. I don't want a divorce,' she stared at him for a moment, her breath catching in her throat at the matter-of-fact way he had spoken.

'That…that's impossible; you know it is.' She took a step backwards away from him, her eyes wide.

He shook his head. 'No, it isn't. It's incredibly simple. I tell my lawyer to go to hell and you do the same with yours.'

'Nothing's changed,' she protested shakily.

'Exactly.' He eyed her sternly.

'What I mean is—'

'I know what you mean,' he interrupted. 'What *I* mean is I was faithful to you before you left and I've been faithful since. No women. Not one. That's the bottom line.'

She stood straight and still, her chin high and her body language saying more than any words could have done.

He stared at her a moment more before saying quietly, 'When I find out who whispered the sweet nothings in your ear, they'll wish they'd never been born. Who was it, Fuzz? Who wanted to destroy us so badly they fed your insecurities with the very thing you most feared?'

'What?' She reached out to lean against the car, needing its solid support. If he had yelled at her she could have taken it in her stride, but the almost tender note in his voice frightened her to death. 'I don't know what you're talking about. I'm not insecure. Just because I'm not the sort of woman to turn a blind eye to—'

'Insecurities which came into being when your mother dumped you in the hands of the social services,' he interrupted again, his voice flat now, and holding a ruthlessness which was more typical of him. 'Insecurities which grew in that damn awful place you were brought up in and which crippled you emotionally. The ones which told you no one could love you or want you or need you, not for ever anyway. Why would they when the one person in all the world who should love you beyond life gave you away like an unwanted gift?'

'Stop it.' Her face was as white as lint. Even her lips had lost their colour. 'Why are you doing this?'

'To kick-start the process of making you wake up,' he said, no apology in his tone. 'I'd been waiting eighteen months for it to happen naturally before I realised I could wait eighteen years—or eighty. I'm not that patient.'

'I hate you.' She stared at him, wounded beyond measure by the things he had said.

'No, you don't,' he said evenly. 'You just think you do.'

She was saved having to make a reply when the front door opened on a delighted screech of her name. 'Marsha! Oh, Marsha, honey.' Hannah's plump bulk fairly flew down the steps, and the next moment Marsha was enfolded in a floral scented embrace that took the breath out of her lungs.

'Don't throttle her, woman.'

She was released to the sound of Taylor's mordant voice and Hannah moved her back a little, staring into her face as she said, 'You're thinner. You're too thin. You're not eating enough.'

'Oh, Hannah.' It was as if she had only seen her the day before, Marsha thought wonderingly. The last eighteen months had been swept away in a moment of time and now she couldn't prevent the tears flowing as she said, 'I've missed you.'

Hannah hugged her again, and there was no reproach in her voice or manner when she said, 'Not as much as I've missed you, child.'

They clung together a moment longer before Taylor's

voice brought them apart once more, saying, 'Much as I hate to mention it, I'm starving. Can we continue the reunion inside?'

'Oh, you, thinking of your stomach at a time like this,' Hannah chided smilingly through her own tears.

Marsha walked up the steps and into the house with her arm in Hannah's, and once in the beautifully light-oak panelled hall the Jamaican housekeeper pushed her in the direction of the drawing room, saying, 'The cocktails are all ready. You go in and sit down a while, and I'll call you through in a few minutes.'

'Thank you, Hannah.' It was Taylor who answered, taking Marsha's arm as he led her into the gracious rose and pale lilac high-ceilinged room which had French windows opening out on to the grounds at the back of the house.

Marsha knew what she would see if she walked over to where antique lace was billowing gently in the slight breeze from the garden. Clipped yews bordering an old stone wall, in front of which was a manicured lawn enclosed by flower beds, and behind it a splendid Edwardian summerhouse now used as a changing room for the rectangular swimming pool of timeless style that Taylor had installed ten years before, when he had bought the house.

She walked over to one of the two-seater sofas dotted about the room and sat down before she said, 'You should have told me you were bringing me here.'

'You wouldn't have agreed to come,' he answered quietly, a silky note in his voice.

'So you tricked me. Clever you.' It was acidic.

He poured a pale pink cocktail, and then one for himself, and it was only after he had handed her the tall fluted glass and sat down himself opposite her that he said, 'Why is it easier to believe lies than the truth? Have you ever asked yourself that?'

'Meaning regarding you and Tanya, I suppose?' she said flatly.

He sat back in his seat, studying her over the rim of his glass. 'Has it never occurred to you that you might be wrong about all this?'

Hundreds, thousands of times, but wishful thinking didn't stand up when confronted by harsh reality. She would never forget the churning of her stomach when she had made that call to Germany, or the sickening feeling when the hotel receptionist had put her through to Taylor's room and the bright, fluttery voice of Tanya had answered. 'No.' She swallowed. It was hard to lie with his eyes on her. 'I might be a fool but I'm not certifiable.'

'I see.' He set down his drink and then steepled his fingers, his gaze never leaving her face for a moment. 'Then we won't waste any more time tonight discussing it. Drink your cocktail.' And he smiled the smile which lit up his face. The rat. The low-down, cheating, lying, philandering rat.

Marsha stared at him, the misery she had been feeling replaced by a healthy dose of anger. How dared he sit there smiling like the cat with the cream when he had all but destroyed her eighteen months ago? Without taking her eyes from his, she set her glass down with a little touch of defiance. 'Is Tanya still working for you?' she asked baldly. He was not going to dictate what they discussed and what they didn't, not after kidnapping her!

'Of course.' He undid his dinner jacket as he spoke, slipping it off and slinging it across the room to another sofa, before loosening his tie so it hung in two thin strands on either side of his throat.

'Of course.' She put a wealth of sarcasm into her voice.

He picked up his glass again, draining it before he added, 'But only for the next month or so, unfortunately. I shall be sorry to lose her; she's a damn good secretary and they don't grow on trees.'

'She's leaving you?' Marsha raised fine eyebrows in what she hoped was a mocking expression. 'Dear, dear. A better offer?'

'Not exactly.' He stood up, moving across to her and handing her her glass again. 'Drink up. There's time for another before Hannah calls us through, and I've ordered a taxi for later.'

She accepted the glass simply because she felt she needed the fortifying effect the alcohol would have on her nerves. It tasted heavenly, but Hannah had always been able to mix a mean cocktail. After two sips, she said, 'If it's not a better offer, why is she going?' Lovers' tiff?

'She's having a baby at the end of September.'

Marsha drank deeply, using the action as an excuse to break the force of his eyes on hers. 'Thank you.' She held out the empty glass with a brittle smile. 'That was lovely.'

'Wasn't it?' he murmured softly. He strolled over to the cocktail cabinet, his movements easy.

Marsha wondered whether Hannah would support her if she demanded to leave. So this was why he had made the move after all this time? Tanya was pregnant. By him? The pain which sliced through her was too severe to continue down that path, so she brushed the possibility aside until she could consider it when she was alone.

'I think her husband wants a little girl; he has two boys from a previous relationship,' Taylor continued with his back to her as he poured two more drinks. 'But I guess all that matters in the long run is that the child is healthy.'

She sat very still as he turned and walked back to her, accepting the drink from him with a slight inclination of her head. So Tanya was married? When had that happened? The other woman had been a Miss when she had left Taylor. Had Tanya been seeing Taylor as well as the man who was now her husband at the time of the Germany trip? Did her husband know she had been more than just a secretary to Taylor at one time? A hundred questions were buzzing in her head, but she couldn't ask any of them.

She raised her head as Taylor took the chair he had vacated, and for a moment her gaze met his. Her breath caught for a second at the look in his eyes. It was brief, and instantly veiled, but for a moment she had seen the inner man, the man she had known in the intimacy of their bed. The vital, vigorous, dynamic lifeforce which was Taylor, a force which let nothing and no one stand in the way of something he wanted. It was this magnetic power which had made her flee that night eighteen months ago, before he had had a chance to convince her that black was white, before that dark, dangerous energy of his reached out and smothered all rational thought and sense.

Contrary to what she'd expected, Taylor said nothing more as they sat and sipped their drinks in a silence which was fairly shrieking. The rich scents from the garden were drifting into the room on the warm breeze and a summer twilight was beginning to fall. The sounds of the birds as they began to settle down for the night and the drone of lazy insects about their business were the only intrusion.

Marsha resisted glancing Taylor's way. She could feel he was watching her, his long lean body stretched out indolently in a very masculine pose, the amber eyes hooded and intense. He hadn't moved a muscle, and yet the very air around them had become sensuous and coaxing. He could do that, she thought crossly, willing herself not to fidget in spite of the ripples of sexual awareness which had caused her nipples to flower and harden and her mouth to become dry. He could seduce by his very presence alone, and it was galling to have to recognise that his power over her body was just the same as it had always been.

She stared into her cocktail glass, determined it wouldn't be her who would break the silence. And she wouldn't mention Tanya West—or whatever her name was now—again either. Pregnant... The rush of emotion was so strong she had to purposely relax her fingers or risk breaking the stem of the glass. There had been a time when she had ached to have Taylor's baby, and it had only been his insistence that they have some time enjoying each other together first that had prevented her from stopping taking the Pill. Of course she hadn't been aware that Taylor was busy 'enjoying' other women too, she reflected sourly.

A minor commotion in the garden involving a great deal of frenzied squawking brought Taylor out of his chair in one smooth, fluid movement. To Marsha's absolute bewilderment, he bent down behind a sofa close to the open French doors, re-emerging a second later with what looked like a child's water gun.

'Taylor?' The question she'd been about to put to him was lost in the furore as he leapt out into the garden, firing as he went in a very personable imitation of James Bond. A moment later a loud yowl was added to the hubbub in the garden.

'Got him.' As Marsha joined Taylor outside, curiosity having got the better of her, he turned to her, satisfaction written all over his handsome face. 'A couple more soakings and he'll get the message.'

'Who will get what message?'

'The neighbourhood tom. He's after the resident blackbird's fledglings in one of the yews. The water doesn't hurt him, but it sure as hell dents his pride when he skulks off like a drowned rat. Any day now and his male ego will acknowledge he can't take any more of this.'

And Taylor would know all about male ego. Marsha was about to voice the thought when a blackbird sailed by their heads in what looked suspiciously like a victory dance. Taylor called after it, 'Right on, buddy! He doesn't stand a chance.'

This was the man who had started and built up a multi-million-pound business before he was thirty. Marsha felt she knew what Alice had felt like in Wonderland.

'Listen.' As she went to speak Taylor moved his head on one side, listening intently.

'What?' she whispered. 'Is the cat back?'

'No.' He grinned at her, slinging the gun over his shoulder as he turned towards the house. 'Hannah's calling us for dinner.'

CHAPTER THREE

THE dinner was wonderful, but Marsha had known it would be. Hannah was an excellent cook. As course followed delicious course, accompanied by a wine which was truly superb, Marsha was aware that Taylor had set himself out to be the perfect dinner companion.

He talked of inconsequential things, his manner easy, but Marsha kept reminding herself she wasn't fooled by his lazy air and lack of aggression. This was Taylor, and she forgot it at her peril. She had lived with this man for eighteen months, and known him for nearly nine months before that, and one thing that time had taught her was that he was single-minded and unapologetically ruthless when he wanted something. And right now that was her.

The dining table had been intimately set for two, complete with candles and roses and scented napkins. In spite of her bulk, Hannah glided in and out with each course, her face beaming whenever Marsha glanced at her but otherwise uncharacteristically silent.

A cold-blooded seduction scene, Marsha told herself, and Taylor had used his charm to obtain Hannah's assistance. What had he told the housekeeper about their break-up? Certainly not the truth; she would bet her life on it.

It was after dessert—a velvety, luxurious, smooth chocolate terrine topped with fresh cream and strawberries—that Marsha decided enough was enough. She had just related an amusing incident which had happened that day at work and he had laughed, the hard angles of his face breaking up into attractive curves. The danger signals had gone off big-time.

What was she *doing*? she asked herself furiously. How on earth had she managed to get herself into this ridiculous position? Taylor had re-entered her life with all the finesse and thoughtfulness of a charging bull elephant, and she had let him get away with bullying her into having dinner with him. And in their marital home at that! She needed her head looking at.

'What's the matter?'

She looked up to meet Taylor's unreadable eyes, trying to disguise the sudden panic in hers by keeping her face deadpan. 'I'm sorry?' she asked coolly, through her whirling dismay.

'Correct me if I'm wrong, but I suspect we're suddenly back to square one.' The dark brows had drawn together. 'Why?'

Did he have any idea how powerfully attractive he was? Marsha moistened dry lips.

But of course he did, she answered silently in the next moment. Born in a high-rise slum to a mother who drank and a father who was rarely around, Taylor had used his devastating looks, charm and rapier-sharp intelligence from an early age.

He had left home at fifteen, started his own sound equipment business at eighteen, with money he had begged and borrowed, and at twenty had been in a position to give Susan—who was four years younger than him—a home, after their mother had died of a drink-related problem and their father had taken himself off for good.

At the tender age of twenty-three he'd had his first million under his belt and more had followed. He was a self-made man, now thirty-five years of age, with a name which was both respected and feared for the ruthlessness it embodied.

But he had never been ruthless with her. The thought came from nowhere, and she countered the weakening effect it had on her resolve. Not outwardly anyway, but then secret affairs were the worst sort of ruthlessness. Susan had been sure there had been others before Tanya, but even if there hadn't, one infidelity was one too many.

'I've no idea what you are talking about,' she said crisply. 'We're not "back" anywhere. We've never moved in the first place. You asked me to dinner because—' She stopped abruptly. Why exactly *had* he asked her?

'Because I wanted to be with you?' he suggested smoothly.

'Because you wanted us to part in a civilised way.' She remembered civilised had been in there somewhere.

'Making it up as you go along.' He smiled, but it didn't reach the magnificent tawny eyes. 'Nothing changes, I see.'

She glared at him. If anyone in this room suffered from a severe aversion to the truth, it wasn't her. 'Now, look here—'

'No, *you* look, my sweet, headstrong, perverse wife.' He had risen with one of the swift animal-like movements characteristic of him, and before she could react he had drawn her to her feet, both hands gripping her elbows as he held her in front of him. 'I intend to talk this through.'

'I don't want to talk,' she protested, angry at the way his nearness was affecting her equilibrium. 'There's nothing to say and no need to talk.'

'Maybe you're right at that.' His eyes had locked on hers, drawing her into the glowing amber as he filled her vision. 'Action speaks louder than words, isn't that what they say?'

She had arched back, but in one expert movement he had drawn her into him, his mouth coming down quickly on hers.

She struggled, but it was like beating herself against solid stone as he held her with the force of his body, his mouth plundering hers. She knew she was fighting herself as much as Taylor—the second his lips had touched hers she wanted him with a passion which frightened her more than anything else could have done. This was the man who had betrayed her, broken her heart and then sailed back into her life as though he had every right to be there. She couldn't, she mustn't, give in to him.

But the desire was as it had always been from the first moment she had met him—clean and hot and senseless. He was the master of the senses, her senses, whether she liked it or not, she thought desperately. He always had been.

The kiss was deep and potent, the taste and smell of him spinning in her head as she fought for control of the need which was raging through her flesh. It had been so long since she had been in his arms like this, and desire was a fire inside her which was spreading however she tried to dampen it down.

His mouth was urgent and hungry, but not cruel. Nevertheless, as she managed to jerk her head away for an instant, she gasped, 'You're hurting me. Let me go.'

Even as his mouth claimed hers again she felt him tense and knew her words had registered. For a moment he continued to hold her, so she could feel every inch of his powerful body, and then, with a low groan, he wrenched his mouth from hers. He was breathing hard, the trembling she'd felt in his body mirrored in hers. She was conscious of his chest rising and falling under the fine linen shirt as he fought for control for one more second, and then suddenly—regretfully—she was free. And now she was fighting an almost overwhelming craving to fling herself into his arms again.

She instinctively hid behind attack being the best defence. 'How dare you manhandle me?' She ignored the hot, insistent flow of desire flowing through her shaking limbs. 'You try anything like that again and I swear I'll scream the place down. Maybe even Hannah would think twice about working for a man who forces women.'

He surveyed her for what seemed like an eternity without speaking, his hands now thrust into the pockets of his trousers. 'Methinks the lady protests too hard.' And then he smiled, as if amused.

He had to be the most infuriating man ever born. Why couldn't he get angry at what she had just said? Instead he stood there looking immensely pleased with life, the arrogant, two-timing, conceited swine. She tried to match his composure when she said, 'Don't flatter yourself, Taylor. I'm counting the minutes, let alone the hours until I'm free of you for good.'

His smile disappeared. She would have liked to have felt triumphant, but merely felt sick at heart. To think they had come to this when it had been so *good*.

The entrance of Hannah, with a tray of coffee and the special shortcake she made—which was utterly delicious and melted in the mouth—silenced further sparring.

Hannah glanced at them both but made no comment,

although the atmosphere was such you didn't need to be the brain of Britain to work out all was not well. Whether the housekeeper had noticed her swollen lips and tousled hair, Marsha wasn't sure, but if she had Hannah was being the soul of discretion—which wasn't like her.

Marsha had sat down as the door had opened, but Taylor remained standing by her chair until Hannah left the room again, at which point he walked over to the window in the dining room and stood looking out into the dark night.

Marsha looked down into her glass and wondered if the excess of wine she'd consumed was making her maudlin. But it wasn't the alcohol. It was the sight of Taylor looking good enough to eat that had her forcing back the tears. She wanted to be over him, she *needed* to be over him, so why couldn't she manage her feelings as she'd learnt to manage the rest of her life?

She could feel the tension within mounting and wondered how much more of his silence she could take. But she wasn't going to speak first. Silly, maybe, perhaps even childish, but she needed every small victory she could get with Taylor.

'Fancy taking our coffees outside?' He turned as he spoke, his tone so perfectly normal and matter-of-fact that Marsha could have floored him. Here was she, tied up in knots and suffering the torment of the damned, and he was Mr Cool.

She shrugged nonchalantly, lifting her eyes to meet his. 'If you like, and then I really will have to go. I've an important meeting first thing tomorrow.'

'Oh, yes?' He raised enquiring eyebrows as he walked over to the table and lifted the coffee pot.

'Jeff—he's my boss and one of the producers—wants

me to discuss ideas for a documentary we've been looking into. His researchers have given me reams of information, but I need to pull it together and sell the concept overall.'

She was unaware of how animated her voice had become as she talked about the work she loved, but he had stopped filling the coffee cups and was giving her his full attention as he said, 'You're his assistant, I take it?'

She nodded. It had been a huge boost to her self-esteem when she had snatched the coveted job from a host of other hopefuls, some of them internal applicants, mainly because Jeff had remembered her from her pre-marriage days. She had come across his path whilst on a training scheme for people who were expected to rise to become producers or managers for a different television company, and although the contact had only been fleeting he had obviously been impressed with her.

It had been her decision, along with a little gentle persuasion from Taylor, to leave the other company after her marriage, mainly because the sort of hours and commitment the five-year training scheme involved could be very antisocial, and she had wanted to be with her new husband as much as possible. In hindsight, it was a decision she bitterly regretted.

Her first at university, in English and Communication Studies, had meant constant hard work and dedication, but it had lifted her into the realm of high-calibre graduates. This had given her a ticket on to the training scheme, at which only a mere handful of the thousands who applied each year were successful. And then she had thrown it all away. But for the lucky break with Jeff she could well have found herself making the tea and sweeping up rather than back in the hub of things.

'I'm pleased for you, Fuzz.'

His quiet voice brought her out of her thoughts and her eyes focused on his sombre face. She stared at him, knowing that certain something which had always used to sizzle between them was still there and hating the power it gave him. She made her voice cool when she said, 'Really?' putting a wealth of disbelief in the one word.

'Uh-huh. Really.' He had crossed his arms over his chest, studying her with those strangely beautiful tawny eyes which had always seemed to look straight into her soul.

'Forgive me, but I find that difficult to believe,' she said, allowing her gaze to freeze.

'I do—forgive you, that is,' he returned comfortably. 'Mainly because I understand now just how fragile and insecure you are beneath that beautiful, resilient exterior.'

Insecure again. If he said that word once more she wouldn't be held responsible for her actions!

'It was a mistake for you to give up your career when we married, but I didn't realise that until it was too late. You needed the sense of self-worth it gave you. I thought I would be enough for you, that I could give you everything you needed, but it was too soon.'

'Cut the psychoanalysis, Taylor,' she said stonily. 'The mistake I made was trusting you; it's as simple as that.'

'Nothing is simple where you are concerned, as I've learnt to my cost.' He finished pouring the coffee as he spoke, seemingly totally unconcerned by her declaration. 'I always thought someone was innocent until proven guilty in this country.' He turned suddenly to face her for an instant. 'Where's your proof, Fuzz?'

Her body jerked as if she had been stung, but although she eyed him hotly she said nothing.

'You won't even do me the courtesy of allowing me to challenge the person who caused the breakdown of our marriage.'

'You can challenge Tanya any day,' she bit back swiftly.

'Tanya is as innocent as I am of all charges.' It was laconic. He placed the cups, sugar and cream, along with the shortbread, on the tray Hannah had left propped against the table. 'Shall we?' He waved his hand towards the garden before picking up the tray.

She walked past him out of the room, continuing down the hall and into the drawing room, whereupon she made her way out of the French doors. The automatic lights clicked on as she stepped on to the patio area beyond which the lawn lay. The sound of the small fountain falling into the lily pond at the side of the patio reminded her of many happy meals eaten alfresco, but she resolutely refused to dwell on the memory.

She walked across to the wicker table and ticking-cushioned chairs she and Taylor had chosen together just after their marriage, when she had persuaded him that eating outside was fun, sitting down facing the yews and old stone wall. The flower beds were a riot of colour, their scent adding to the beauty all around her, and the sky was black velvet, pierced with stars.

She didn't speak as Taylor placed the tray on the table and sat down, but as he went to add cream and sugar to her cup she said, 'I take mine black now, thank you.'

He quirked a brow. 'The cream and sugar queen?'

'We drink coffee all day at work, and I've got used

to it black.' It was a silly thing, but she was pleased she'd surprised him.

'I can see I mustn't assume anything,' he drawled mockingly, making her feel as though she was being puerile for the sake of it.

But she *had* changed in the last eighteen months, she thought militantly, and drinking her coffee black was the least of it. 'Quite so,' she responded evenly, as though she hadn't caught the inflection in his voice, and she ignored the slight smile twisting his lips with an aplomb she was proud of.

There were six chairs grouped round the table, but he had chosen to sit in the one next to her rather than opposite, as she had expected, and now he was so close his shoulder was almost brushing hers. With an effort, Marsha relaxed her body, determined not to give him the satisfaction of knowing how tense she was.

Some moments had ticked by before she said, 'What did you mean when you said you'd known where I was every minute since we split up?' It had been at the back of her mind all evening, she realised now with a dart of surprise as she heard herself speak.

'Exactly that.'

She wasn't going to let him get away with being so succinct. 'That's not an answer,' she said, finishing her coffee.

'Of course it is.' He turned his head, the amber light on her face, but she kept her gaze on the shadowed garden. 'You didn't really think I would just let you walk out of the house and my life, did you?'

Her stomach trembled. 'Who…? How…?'

She didn't know quite how to put it, but he seemed to understand what she was trying to say. He shifted slightly in his chair, his long legs stretched out in front of him, and as she caught a faint whiff of his aftershave a hundred nerves went haywire.

'I employed someone, okay?' he said mildly.

No, not okay! *Mega* not okay. 'You *employed* someone?' she said, so shrilly a number of birds protested in the trees surrounding the garden as their slumber was interrupted. 'You had me watched? Like…like a criminal?'

'Don't be childish,' he said calmly as her eyes met his. 'I wanted to make sure you were all right, that was all. You are my wife, my responsibility.'

'The hell I am!'

He clicked his tongue disapprovingly, shaking his head at her. She deeply regretted there was no coffee left in her cup to fling at him. 'I would like to leave now.' She stood to her feet, her eyes blazing.

'Sure.' To her absolute amazement, Taylor rose lazily. 'The taxi's been outside for the last few minutes. I didn't think you'd want to be too late on a working day.'

'Who was he? This guy you had spy on me?' Much as she would have liked to storm off with her nose in the air, she really wanted to know.

'He was a she, and from one of the most reputable firms in the country.' He looked at her squarely. 'And there was no question of spying. She merely checked now and again that you weren't in any trouble, that everything was okay. That was it.'

'And who I saw and where I went and with whom?' Indignation lit her eyes and flushed her cheeks.

He was magnificently unperturbed. 'Of course. You are my wife.'

'We are *separated*.'

'You're still my wife, Marsha.' The use of her name

checked her even more than the tone of his voice, which had suddenly chilled.

She looked into amber eyes which had become as dangerous as those of a big cat, and just as hard. 'I shall never forgive you for this,' she said shakily. 'To have me watched, put under surveillance as though *I'm* the one in the wrong—' She wished with all her heart she *had* met someone in the last months, gone out on a date or two, flirted a little—anything to puncture that giant ego.

'Then it is merely another crime to be added to the list, yes?' He shrugged as though bored.

'And you obviously don't care about any of your crimes, right?' she snapped, furiously angry with his offhand manner and lack of remorse.

'If you are referring to my supposed affair with Tanya, I plead innocent to all charges, remember?'

She glared at him, wondering how it was that he could so get under her skin, even when she knew exactly what he was playing at. She ought to be able to ignore his arrogance, but it grated on her unbearably. 'I want the bloodhound called off.'

'I doubt the very attractive woman concerned would appreciate being labelled a dog.'

He was laughing at her! She stared into the hard face, quivering with righteous indignation. 'I can think of worse things to call her,' she said forcefully.

'I don't doubt it.'

'Does she know the sort of man she's working for?'

'I think so.' He was regarding her lazily. 'More to the point, do you?'

'Only too well.'

'Now, *that* I doubt.' He caught her upper arms in his hands, holding her in front of him and looking deep into her eyes as he said, 'But before I'm finished you will know, Marsha. That's a promise.'

'Let go of me.' She stood rigid in his grasp, glaring furiously up at him. 'I don't appreciate being subjected to brute force.'

'Brute force?' His eyes pierced her with laser brightness. 'There's times I wonder what planet you're on.'

His complete refusal to accept any blame for his actions made her see red. 'You're the lowest of the low—you know that, don't you?' she hissed bitterly. 'I hate you—'

Anything else she might have said was cut off by the simple expedient of his mouth on hers. She knew enough not to struggle this time, willing herself to show no feeling at all as he brought all his sexual experience to the fore in a kiss that was tender and erotic and deep in turn. He gently probed her mouth until her lips parted for him of their own volition as resistance drained from her, in spite of all her efforts to remain unmoved.

He was just too good at this, she thought feverishly. He always had been. In the early days she had been enchanted to find a man who kissed like Taylor, who made it into an art. The trouble was it had left her with no defences, no barriers to the response he could always bring forth with seemingly effortless skill.

She knew she was melting against him, and yet she could no more have stopped her body's response than she could have stopped breathing, and the past and the present were forgotten as the magic that was his mouth took her senses. Taylor shifted his stance slightly to take more of her weight, one arm going round her waist and the other moving to take a handful of her hair as he pulled her head back gently for greater access to her mouth. The position and feel of him brought a torrent of memories to mind, and all of them good.

His tongue curled round hers, probing in a way that sent tremors throughout her whole body, and then his mouth moved to one earlobe, nibbling gently. Heat was flowing in her veins, intensified by his tongue as it traced a delicate path in and around her ear in a sensual pattern that had her legs trembling.

Her eyes were closed now, colours and sensation merging as she gave herself utterly to the bewitching assault. She could feel his arousal, hard against her softness, and it added to the pleasure she was experiencing. Her body felt as if it was one hot, sensual nerve.

'You're so beautiful, so delicious.' The soft whisper came at a time when he was caressing her aching breasts with sure fingers, each light touch sending electricity bolts right down to her toes. 'I could eat you, devour you.'

And she wanted him to. She couldn't stop her hips moving against him in an invitation that was as old as time, and moans shuddered through her body as the scent of him surrounded her in an intoxicating bubble.

He was powerfully muscled, without an ounce of surplus flesh, his body hard and uncompromisingly male, and as her hands roamed over his wide shoulders and strong chest her desire reached fever pitch. She felt the cool night air on her breasts and realised he must have undone the tiny mother-of-pearl buttons on her jacket without her being aware of it. But it was when his hands cradled her breasts, his fingers having pushed the filmy lace of her bra out of the way, that she found the strength to push him away.

'No.' She took a step backwards, her legs shaking so

much she felt they wouldn't hold her. 'I don't want this.'

He made no move towards her, merely raising a dark eyebrow as he said, 'That's not what your body is saying.'

She stared at him, forced to admit to herself that her whole body was so sensitised by his lovemaking that every move he made registered on her nervous system. 'I'm not saying that I'm not physically attracted to you,' she said carefully, 'but that is something quite different.'

'You've lost me.' He sounded tolerant, and she didn't trust that. Tolerance was not one of Taylor's attributes.

'We're no longer an item, Taylor. That's what I'm saying,' she said firmly.

'We never were an "item", Fuzz. We were married, remember?' He didn't sound quite so tolerant now. 'Or should I say we *are* married.'

She did up the buttons on her jacket as swiftly as her trembling hands would permit, furious with herself for giving in so easily to what was clearly a ploy on his part. He thought he only had to turn on the charm and she would fall at his feet, she thought caustically, ignoring the little voice in her head which added nastily that he was quite right.

'I think it's high time I went home.' She raised her chin as she spoke, desperate to hide the burning sense of shame that had flooded every part of her.

'You are home.'

'You know exactly what I mean.'

'You mean you want to go back to that lonely little box you inhabit, right?'

She reared up like a scalded cat at the insult to the home she had so carefully put together. 'You say the taxi is waiting?' she asked, with a cool dignity she was very pleased about afterwards, when she thought about it.

'That it is.' The amusement was back in his voice, and nothing could have been more guaranteed to hit her on the raw.

'Then thank you for dinner,' she said icily, 'but I really do have to leave now.'

'I'll tell Hannah you're leaving. You *were* going to say goodbye to her, weren't you?' he added disparagingly.

'Of course I was.' She frowned at him, hurt that he could suggest otherwise. 'I've no quarrel with Hannah.'

'She'll be most relieved to hear it,' he drawled mockingly.

'I hate you.'

'That's the third time you've said that today. Are you trying to convince me or yourself?'

CHAPTER FOUR

MARSHA awoke very early the next morning, before it was light, after a sleep which had been troubled and restless. After making herself coffee, she took a mug out on to the balcony along with her duvet, snuggling under its folds as she sat and watched the dawn break.

Taylor had insisted on accompanying her home in the taxi the night before, despite all her heated protests, but contrary to her expectations hadn't done so much as hold her hand on the journey back to the bedsit. After telling the driver to wait, he had escorted her to the door of the building—again with her protests ringing in his ears—and then up the stairs to her floor.

She had faced him defiantly then, waiting for the move she'd been sure he would make after that scorching kiss back at his house in Harrow, but he had merely nodded to her without smiling once she had opened her front door, wished her goodnight and left.

Which left her where? she asked herself now, her tired eyes searching the pink and mother-of-pearl sky in front of her as though it could provide an answer. Had he admitted defeat? Was he going to leave her alone now she had made it crystal-clear how she still felt?

She drained the mug, setting it down on the floor beside the chair before letting her head fall back against the cane as she shut her eyes. She *was* right about all this—him, their marriage, Tanya, everything—wasn't she? But of course she was. She had to be. The misery of the last eighteen months couldn't be for nothing. He had slept with Tanya in Germany, even if he hadn't done so before, and from what Susan had said there had been a before. Several befores.

But he had seemed so...plausible. She opened her eyes again. The hum of traffic and sounds from the street beyond the cul-de-sac were louder now the city had begun to wake up and go about its business. But then he'd always been able to make anyone believe anything. That was one of the gifts he had which had shot him from obscurity to extreme wealth in such a short time.

She wriggled restlessly, drawing her cold toes into her hands under the duvet. The day was due to be another hot one, but the morning air was decidedly cool.

She still loved him. The truth which had haunted her sleep wouldn't be denied in the harsh light of day. She would always love him. The love which had been such a blessing when they were together and happy would forever be a millstone round her neck. And because she loved him so much she could never go back to him.

She rose, her movements jerky with pain, and, leaving the duvet on the chair, strode back into the room to make herself another coffee.

She had been aware of Taylor with every cell in her body last night, and that alone told her she had to be strong. She had done her days and nights of weeping for what might have been. That was over. Maybe if she had been a different type of woman, one who was able to turn a blind eye to her man's little liaisons, perhaps, or if she hadn't loved him quite so much, things might have been different. As it was, he would destroy her.

She didn't intend to live the rest of her life looking about her for the next notch on Taylor's bedpost to emerge, or, worse still, become like one or two women she'd known in the past, who had gone through their partner's pockets every night looking for signs that they were playing away from home.

She cupped her cold hands round the hot mug of coffee, inhaling its fragrance even as the chill within deepened. She had had her time of being naive and starry-eyed, of thinking that there really was such a thing as happy endings in this tough, dog-eat-dog world, but she knew better now. And she would not make the same mistake again.

Taylor had left her without a word last night, and that was for the best. She saw that now. He had got to her despite all her efforts to keep him at bay, he had breached the wall she had built around her emotions as easily as he had always done, but she would make sure it did not happen again. She wasn't quite sure how she would manage it, but she would—if they met again, that was.

She drank the coffee scalding hot, sitting at the breakfast bar, before marching on to the balcony and retrieving the duvet from the chair.

Once the bedsit was put in order, she showered and washed her hair, making up her face quickly and expertly before dressing in a pale lilac cotton suit with a boatneck jacket and short pencil-slim skirt. She didn't normally dress so formally for the office, but with the forthcoming meeting in mind she knew it would be expected.

It was still only half-past six when she left the house, but she wanted to clear her head by walking to work, and arriving so early would give her plenty of time to be word-perfect for the meeting at ten o'clock.

It was a beautiful morning, the streets already spangled by sunlight but the chill of the night causing the city air to smell clean and fresh for once. It was on mornings like these that she and Taylor had eaten breakfast in their bathrobes on the patio, the twitter of the birds and the drone of the odd aircraft overhead mingling with their laughter and the smell of warm croissants, fresh from Hannah's oven. She hadn't been able to enjoy a croissant since she had left.

She frowned, annoyed with herself for letting the memory intrude on the morning. She had to be focused on her work and nothing else, she knew that, so no more mawkish thoughts. She nodded determinedly at the declaration, striding out with renewed purpose.

Her steps slowed fractionally as she approached the television building, inner turmoil reasserting itself as she faced the prospect that her marriage would soon be the current news on the gossip grapevine. But she couldn't worry about that, and it was no one's business but hers after all. She would explain to Nicki, she owed the other woman that, but other than with her secretary she would not discuss the matter, should anyone have the temerity to raise it.

Once in her office she kicked off her high-heeled shoes, hung her jacket on the back of her chair, and within moments had become immersed in all the Baxter paperwork.

Nicki arrived prompt at eight-thirty, at which time Marsha suggested they lunch together and have a chat, but other than that she continued to pore over the files on her desk.

At ten she sailed into the meeting, looking confident and self-assured, and by half-past she knew she had won everyone over—everyone except Penelope, that was. The other woman's cold blue eyes had been the first thing she'd seen when she had entered the boardroom, and after Penelope had cut her dead when she had smiled at her, Marsha knew she wasn't the flavour of the month.

'I just don't know if we should take on a conglomerate like Manning Dale on such…scant information.' Penelope looked round the table reflectively, her thin eyebrows raised. 'We don't want another lawsuit thrown at us so soon after the last one. I mean, how do we *know* the big boys stepped on Charles Baxter to make him sign away his business? And even if—*if*,' she emphasised, her scarlet-painted lips lingering on the word for a moment, 'they did, it doesn't necessarily follow they've done the same thing before. What we have here is a number of statements, all from people with axes to grind.'

'I disagree,' Jeff North said firmly, his face rather than his voice expressing some surprise that Penelope was taking this tack on what to him was a cut and dried matter. 'From the facts and figures Marsha has presented this morning it's obvious dirty deals have shadowed Manning Dale's success from day one, but this last scam with Baxter ended in a man's death. We need to bring this into the public arena. That's what we're here for.'

'Hmmm.' Penelope glanced at the other top executive in the room, who was effectively Jeff's boss. 'Do you think Marsha has collected enough data, Tim? My fear is that her…enthusiasm for the story has made her a little slapdash.'

Timothy Cassell joined his hands in front of him on the table, studying them for a second or two before he looked up. He had worked with Penelope for more than a decade and knew her very well. For some reason she was gunning for Jeff's assistant, and when she was like this she could be as awkward as blazes. The story was a good one, and they all knew it, but delaying it for a week or two on the pretext of collecting more information wouldn't be the end of the world. Certainly he had no wish to get on Penelope's bad side. They had a policy of 'you scratch my back and I'll scratch yours' which had worked exceedingly well over the years.

He cleared his throat, avoiding looking at Marsha's burning face as he said, 'See what else you can find out, by all means, and we'll look at it again in a couple of weeks. Now, is there anything else while we're all together?'

'Well, yes, this new equipment we've been looking at? I've got the quotes in now, and one in particular is most attractive. Kane International?' And then, as if suddenly realising she was speaking out of turn, Penelope turned to the others in the room, saying sweetly, 'Thank you, everyone. I don't think we need to keep you any longer.'

'What was all that about?' Once they were in the lift, returning to their more lowly floor, Jeff scratched his head in bewilderment as he glanced at Marsha's hot face. 'There's enough information in this lot to satisfy anyone.'

'I think it's my fault.' Marsha had decided that prevarication was pointless. 'Penelope found out I was married yesterday, and was offended she hadn't been informed of the full situation before.'

'You told her?'

'Not exactly.' Marsha took a deep breath. 'The Kane of Kane International is my husband, Jeff. He was here yesterday with Penelope.'

'Ah…'

Much as she would have liked to say Penelope's spite had not affected her, Marsha sat and seethed for the rest of the morning. She had been unfairly criticised and held up as negligent and it was all Taylor's fault, she told herself furiously, refusing to acknowledge the little voice inside which said she was being a mite unfair. But if he hadn't announced they were married yesterday to all and sundry Penelope wouldn't be any the wiser right now and the Baxter story—the first project Jeff had given her sole responsibility for—would be in the bag. His pique at her attempt to cold-shoulder him at the cocktail party yesterday had resulted in her looking a fool this morning in front of everyone. It just wasn't *fair*. But then when had fairness ever been in Taylor's vocabulary? She loathed him, absolutely and utterly *loathed* him. Penelope too. If ever a pair were made for each other, they were.

By lunchtime Marsha had the beginnings of a major headache drumming away behind her eyes, and was as tense as piano wire. She was aware of the small hurried glances Nicki had been giving her ever since she and Jeff had returned from the meeting, but hadn't given her secretary a chance to engage her in conversation once she had informed her that the Baxter story was not yet approved.

Now, as Nicki said carefully, 'We can do lunch another day if you'd rather, Marsha?' she suddenly felt enormously guilty.

'No, not at all.' She forced a smile. 'And I'm sorry for being like a bear with a sore head all morning. Come on, let's go now—and if we're late back, who cares?'

'Fighting talk.' Nicki grinned at her.

To make up for her reluctance, Marsha decided to treat Nicki to lunch at Lyndons—a plush little restaurant a short taxi ride away. Once they had arrived, and were seated at a table for two with an open bottle of wine between them, Marsha relaxed back in her seat with a long sigh. 'Wine in the lunch hour,' she said ruefully. 'I'm slipping, and dragging you down with me.'

'Drag away,' Nicki said with relish as she took a hefty swig at her glass. 'And don't worry about the Baxter story. Everyone knows it's a good one and that Penelope is just having one of her turns.'

'It's the reason for the turn that's bothering me more than the story,' Marsha said soberly.

'Him?' Nicki was nothing if not intuitive.

Marsha nodded. Suddenly she found herself telling Nicki all of it—something she hadn't planned to do at all. She even related her upbringing in the children's home, the two failed attempts at being adopted, which had occurred mainly because she had been convinced her mother would come back for her, her inability to make close friends after her best friend at the home had been adopted and had never contacted her again—the whole story. This between mouthfuls of smoked salmon salad with potato rosti and horseradish cream, followed by lemon chicken and wild rice with courgette strips and peppers. She finished as they were waiting for the dessert menu.

'Wow…' Nicki had shaken her head at regular intervals throughout the account. Now she astounded Marsha by leaning over the table and hugging her with such genuine warmth and sympathy it brought tears to Marsha's eyes. 'And you're still only twenty-seven.'

Nicki hadn't meant to be funny. Whether it was the other girl's face, which was so concerned it was comedic, or the amazed note in Nicki's voice, or yet again the half-bottle of wine, Marsha wasn't sure, but she was relieved to find herself laughing rather than crying. 'I feel decades older,' she admitted ruefully. 'Especially today. I was just getting my life back and he has to turn up again.'

'Some men are like that,' Nicki said, with her vast knowledge of just one. 'Especially when they look as good as he does. They think they just have to snap their fingers and women fall into their lap like ripe plums.'

'He doesn't even have to snap his fingers,' Marsha said truthfully.

Dessert was a wonderful caramelised lemon and orange tart, which they followed with coffee and the restaurant's special homemade truffles. By the time Marsha paid the bill, she knew she had found a wealth of affection and friendliness in the other woman.

She had never had a sister, she reflected as the two of them walked out into the bright sunny afternoon, but if she had she could imagine her being just like Nicki.

It was as they were riding back in the taxi that Nicki said thoughtfully, 'You *are* absolutely positive that this person who told you about Tanya and said there had been others couldn't have had an ulterior motive for lying?'

Marsha nodded. It was the same thought which had occurred to her more than once since last night, but each time she had known she was clutching at straws. She didn't know why she had not told Nicki it was Taylor's sister who had informed on him—it was the only thing she had kept back. Perhaps it was because she had promised Susan she wouldn't divulge her name to Taylor, although there was no chance of Nicki ever telling him.

'You don't have to say a name, but was it a woman?' When Marsha nodded again, Nicki frowned. 'Having seen the man, I'd say there could be an element of doubt there, then.'

Marsha dragged in a deep breath and expelled it resignedly. She'd have to tell her or Nicki would be like a dog with a bone. 'It was his sister, Susan,' she said quietly. 'And she adores him and he, her. So, no motive.'

Nicki glanced at her, her frown deepening. She said nothing, but suggested volumes.

'What?' Marsha stared at the other woman.

'You've never lived in a family environment so you might have an idealised view of siblings,' Nicki said flatly. 'Believe me, being a sister or a brother doesn't automatically qualify you for instant sainthood. There's all sorts of undercurrents in the human psyche, and siblings can bring out the worst in other siblings. When I got a 2.1 at uni, and my sister got a 2.2 two years later, she didn't speak to me for six months.'

'We're talking marriage break-up here, Nicki. Not someone being miffed because of a grade in a degree.'

'Oh, believe me, I could tell you worse stories. Not about my sister,' Nicki added hurriedly, as latent loyalty kicked in, 'but rivalry and jealousy can be at their most intense in families.'

'He's been like mother and father to her all her life,' Marsha argued vehemently. 'She worships the ground he walks on. Even her husband has to take second place to Taylor.'

'Really?' Nicki wrinkled her nose. 'Unhealthy.'

'And she was great to me from day one. She was even my maid of honour.'

'Doesn't mean a thing,' Nicki stated evenly. 'Now, I'm not saying she lied, Marsha, but it's not impossible. Nothing is. At least consider the possibility.'

'Why?' said Marsha, and her brows came together in a perplexed frown at the other girl's doggedness.

'Because you still love him,' Nicki said very quietly. 'And being brought up as you were means there's a whole chunk of experience missing, and that makes you vulnerable.'

'Don't say I'm insecure,' Marsha warned fiercely.

'The word will never pass my lips.'

The rest of the day passed in a whirl of trying to catch up on what she'd missed in the morning as she sat and fumed at Penelope's cavalier treatment of her work. By seven o'clock everyone she normally worked with had gone, and the headache—which the wine had not improved at lunchtime and which she had kept at bay all afternoon with medication—was now a persistent drumming, sending hot flashes of pain into her brain.

When she emerged from the building into the warm June evening she winced as bright sunlight met her eyes, but a search of her handbag revealed she had left her sunglasses at home. Wonderful. The day had just got better and better and looked as if it was going to end on a high note, she thought darkly, the noise of the traffic seeming to roar through her aching head.

'Do you always work this late?'

Her pulse gave a mighty leap and she caught her breath, turning her head to see Taylor standing a yard or so to her right. He was dressed in black jeans and a short-sleeved shirt the colour of his eyes, and he looked wonderful. He smiled at her surprise, his strong white teeth a contrast to his tanned skin.

She thought about her answer for a second or two, instead of coming out with her first response of, What are you doing here? And, considering the headache and the sort of day she'd had, she was rather pleased with the coolness of her voice when she said, 'You should know, surely, with little Miss Private Detective keeping you up to date?'

'Ow.' The devastating smile turned into a grin in which there wasn't a trace of remorse. 'I should have expected that one.'

And he needn't try his charm on her either! He was going to get a nice juicy contract, courtesy of a plainly besotted Penelope, and she was going to get a couple of weeks of frustration, trying to dig up more data when everyone knew all avenues had been exhausted and it wasn't necessary anyway. A shaft of white-hot pain shot through her head and exploded out of her eyes, causing her to visibly wince.

'What's wrong?' The grin had vanished and his voice was soft and deep as he took her arm, drawing her out of the way of other pedestrians and shielding her with his body as they stood at the side of the building.

'Don't.' She shook off his hand, refusing the physical contact. 'It's just a headache, that's all.'

He took in her white face and the blue shadows of exhaustion under her eyes. 'How did the meeting go?' he asked quietly.

'Great.' She stared straight at him. 'Penelope accused me of slackness and implied I wasn't up to the job in front of everyone when she knows full well the story's a hot one. A none too subtle punishment for yesterday. Consequently the story's on hold for a couple of weeks.'

'That's not the end of the world, is it?'

This from a man who had to have everything flowing like clockwork in his work, down to the last 'i' being dotted the second he demanded it. 'Right now, yes, it is,' she said flatly. 'Not that I would expect you to understand for a minute. Your girlfriend is a nasty piece of work, and I resent being made to look a fool simply because I'm your wife—not that that will be the case for much longer.'

His expression altered as he absorbed her words. 'One, Penelope is not my girlfriend. Two, I understand your frustration perfectly. Three, you need a bath, then a light supper, followed by some medication to knock you out, and a cool dark room to sleep the effects off. Agreed?'

It sounded wonderful, but she wasn't about to tell him she didn't have the luxury of a bath in her tiny shower room, or that her fridge boasted nothing more than a wilting lettuce and half a carton of cottage cheese which had probably passed its sell-by date. 'Quite.' She nodded carefully. She wasn't too sure her head wouldn't fall off with any vigorous movement. 'So if you'll excuse me I'll be off home.'

'You don't intend to walk, feeling like you do?'

Not with Taylor in tow. 'I'm going to get a taxi,' she said tersely, his statement about Penelope a massive question mark in her mind. She needed to be somewhere quiet and *think*.

'No need.' He smiled sunnily. 'My car's parked over there. I can have you home in two jiffs.'

'Taylor, how can I put this? I don't want to ride in your car any more than I want to find you waiting for me when I come out of work.' It wasn't true, but he didn't know that. She watched two young girls who couldn't have been more than seventeen or eighteen do a doubletake as they caught sight of him, and hated him for it. Which made her fit for the funny farm, she thought wearily.

'You've a blinding headache and need to get home quickly. I have a car parked ten yards away.' He tilted his head expressively. 'Seems pretty straightforward to me.'

Lots of things seemed straightforward to him, but it did not mean that they were. She wanted to argue, but she was too tired, too muzzy-headed, too heartsore. Suddenly it seemed a whole lot simpler just to allow him to take her home and be done with it. 'Okay.'

'Okay?' He was surprised by the capitulation and it showed.

'I can appreciate logic when it's explained so well,' she said with veiled sarcasm, deciding however bad she felt she wasn't going to make it easy for him.

However, once she was in the safe confines of the car, and the rest of the busy, whirling, hellishly loud world was shut out, the temptation to shut her aching eyes was too strong to resist. The painkillers she had taken at regular intervals during the afternoon—probably *too* regular, she admitted silently—were telling on her. She felt leaden-limbed and exhausted, along with slightly nauseous and dizzy.

'That's right, shut your eyes.' Taylor's voice was no more than a soothing rumble at her side. 'I'll have you home in no time.'

She was not aware she had fallen asleep, but when she heard the murmur of voices and felt a gentle hand rousing her she looked up into Hannah's anxious face and realised she must have been out for the count. She also realised—a touch belatedly—that the home Taylor had referred to had not been her bedsit.

Through the pounding in her head, Marsha glanced out of the open door of the car and saw the steps leading up to Taylor's front door. She groaned. 'I want to go home.'

'You are home.' Taylor's face appeared at the side of Hannah's and it was grim. 'And you're not well. You were sleeping so deeply there I had to check your pulse a couple of times to make sure you were still breathing. What the hell have you been taking, anyway?'

'Just aspirin. And paracetamol. Oh, and one of the researchers gave me a couple of pills she takes for migraines.'

'Give me strength.' It was terse. 'I married a junkie.' And then, as Hannah whispered something, she heard him say, 'Flu, headache or whatever. She needs looking after.'

Marsha wanted to object when he lifted her bodily out of the car, but the effort it would take wasn't worth it. She was aware of Taylor carrying her up the stairs, and of then being placed in a comfortable bed which knocked the spots off her sofabed in the bedsit. But it was when she felt her shoes being taken off and then her jacket that she found the will to open her eyes and protest. 'Don't... I can do it.'

'Don't try my patience.'

'Where's Hannah?'

'Fixing an omelette.'

His hands were firm and sure, but not unkind—not until she tried to push him away, when he gave a none too gentle tap at her fingers. 'We're man and wife, for crying out loud. I've undressed you before.'

'That was different.'

'And how.'

She gave up. She couldn't argue. You had to be *compos mentis* to argue, and it had finally dawned on her that in her anxiety to stifle her headache and prove to all and sundry she was efficient and totally on the ball—whatever Penelope might imply—she had definitely overdone the medication.

Naked as the day she was born, she snuggled into fresh-scented linen covers and was asleep as soon as Taylor's hands left her body.

How soon she was awoken again by a quiet-voiced Hannah she didn't know, but the housekeeper gently plumped the pillows behind her after Marsha groggily sat up to take the tray the other woman was holding. 'You eat that all up, honey.' Once the pillows were sorted, Hannah stood back to gaze at her. 'I daresay you haven't eaten all day, huh?'

'I had a huge lunch,' Marsha protested weakly through the thumping in her head.

Hannah's three chins went down into her neck as her eyebrows rose in the universal expression of disbelief, but Marsha was not up to arguing. She stared down at an omelette done to moist fluffiness beside three thin slices of Hannah's home-cured ham, and knew she couldn't eat a thing.

Hannah, apparently, was not of the same persuasion. 'I'm staying right here till all that's gone,' she warned. 'Boss's instructions.'

'I'm not a child.' Marsha was stung into retaliation.

'Sure you're not, honey.' A fork was placed in her hand and Hannah beamed at her.

Marsha sighed and started to eat, surprised to find that she could clear the plate before sliding back down under the covers again. She was asleep before Hannah left the room.

CHAPTER FIVE

IT WAS the enormous sense of well-being which first registered the next morning as Marsha began to float from layers of soft billowy warmth. She was neither fully asleep nor fully awake, too comfortable and content to move or think. She just luxuriated in the deep tranquillity and peace her mind and body were resting in.

She sighed softly, the caress on her skin part of her dreamlike state and no more threatening than the stroking of a butterfly's wing. The pleasure was tantalising, teasing her senses with half-remembered stirrings which grew sweeter and more potent as she lazily embraced them.

Her body felt fluid, with heat beginning to pulse in time with the erotic rippling over her flesh, and she moaned, her half-open lips captured in the next moment in a kiss that was teasing and tangible. Suddenly she was wide awake.

'Good morning, sweet wife.'

She stared at Taylor, the thick curtain of sleep lifted but her mind refusing to accept for the moment that he was real. And then it all came rushing back—the headache, the pills, and the drive to the house—and she realised to her consternation that the covers were rumpled to one side and she was wearing nothing at all.

'You were touching me.' She made a grab for the duvet, horrified that he had been making love to her without her knowledge. Bringing the cover up to her chin, she eyed him hotly. 'That's despicable.'

He was sitting on the side of the bed and made no effort to deny the charge, merely smiling slowly as he said, 'You taste the same, like warm honey.'

Her heart was racing, less with anger than the pleasure his hands and mouth had called forth so effortlessly, which was still sending needles of desire into every pulse. 'You're the lowest of the low.'

'Why? Because I like to touch and look at my wife?'

'You knew I was asleep.' She glared at him, refusing to acknowledge how the smell and feel of him affected her. 'That's as bad as a peeping Tom.'

'Maybe.' If he agreed with her it didn't bother him an iota. 'But you looked so tempting lying there, and I've never pretended to be a saint. Mortal man can only take so much when confronted with Aphrodite at—' he consulted the gold Rolex on his tanned wrist '—eleven o'clock in the morning.'

'What?' The mention of the time deflected her wrath, as he had known it would. 'It can't be eleven o'clock.' She made a move to spring out of bed and then remembered she was naked. 'Why didn't someone wake me, for goodness' sake? I have a meeting first thing this morning, and a report which has to be on Jeff's desk by noon. I can't believe—'

'Calm down.'

It was the last straw. He could sit there as calm as a cucumber—or was it as cool as a cucumber? She couldn't remember now, but it was all the same—and act as though she should be pleased to discover she was hours late for the office. 'Where are my clothes?' she asked stonily, forcing herself not to give way and yell at him.

'In Hannah's tender care. She thought your suit needed pressing. Of course you have a wardrobe full, still in our room,' he reminded her innocently, before adding, 'How's the head this morning?'

'Fine. I told you last night, it was just a headache. If you had let me walk home—'

'You wouldn't have made it. Not with all the stuff you'd pumped into yourself.'

He made her sound like a drug addict, and she resented it bitterly—that and the fact that he was right. She looked into his face now and saw he was watching her intently, his eyes like polished amber, with a disturbing gleam at the back of them. She swallowed, feeling hot and flustered. 'Thank you,' she said grudgingly, 'for taking care of things.'

'My pleasure.' The carved lips twitched a little.

'But I need to phone the office and explain why I'm late.'

'You aren't late. You're having the day off because you are ill, probably because they are working you too hard. I phoned and spoke to Jeff first thing.'

She stared at him, her expression altering as she absorbed his words. 'You had no right to do that.' Her voice rose with her indignation. 'Not without asking me first.'

'You were asleep,' he pointed out mildly, 'and I thought you'd just thanked me for taking care of things?'

'This is different.' She wished he would stand up and move away. It was more disconcerting than she could express having him sitting inches away from her, fully dressed, when she was stark naked under the questionable protection of the bedcover.

'You would rather have let them think you just hadn't bothered to call in?' he asked with a puzzled frown.

She counted silently to ten. 'What exactly did you say?'

'Exactly?' He shut his eyes for an infinitesimal moment, as though he was trying to recall the conversation, but Marsha was not fooled. That computer brain forgot nothing—ever. 'Merely that you were taken ill last night and would not be fit to work today. I said I would phone before five this evening with an update,' he added helpfully.

Great. Just great. Now Jeff would be thinking all sorts of things—mainly about whose bed she had spent the night in—and she really couldn't blame him. Would he be discreet? She was not sure.

'Stop frowning.' His deep husky voice had laughter somewhere at the back of it, although the chiselled face was perfectly serious. 'You'll have wrinkles before you're thirty at this rate.'

'I have some already,' she snapped back curtly. And the odd grey hair, although she was not about to point that out.

'Not that I can see.' He bent forward on the pretence of looking more closely, invading her air space with the warmth and scent of his body.

The muscled strength that padded his chest and shoulders was very apparent under the thin silk of the shirt he was wearing, and Marsha had to force herself not to wriggle back against the pillows.

She would *not* give him the satisfaction of knowing how much he bothered her, she told herself furiously. But she wished she had had time to at least brush her teeth and wash her face before he had decided to come in. She tried to stop looking at his mouth. It was a very sexy, cynical mouth, and had always had the power to make her bones melt.

'If you would like to tell Hannah I'm ready for my clothes, I can at least make an appearance before lunch and work on the report for this afternoon,' she said stiffly.

'I wouldn't—like to tell Hannah, that is,' he said without moving an inch.

'Taylor, I'm going into the office today.'

'Marsha, you are not.'

His use of her Christian name warned her that, however calm and laid-back he appeared, he meant business, as did the glint in his eyes.

'This is quite ridiculous. You can't keep me here against my will and—'

Anything else she might have said was swallowed up as his mouth came down quickly on hers, a deft turn of his body bringing his hands either side of her slim shape as he pinned her beneath him. She wriggled and tried to fight him, only to realise that any movement brought the duvet dangerously close to slipping right down her body. She stopped squirming and immediately the kiss became subtly deeper, his mouth and tongue doing incredible things to her.

Heat was racing through her bloodstream and she felt the length and power of his arousal, her nerve-endings becoming sensitised as he moved his hips over her shape in a way which forced her to recognise his dominance. But his mouth was all persuasion. He probed, he sipped, he nipped, moving down from her lips when he felt her trembling submission and heard the little moans she couldn't hide, to rain burning kisses on her throat, her neck and the smooth silky skin beneath.

Her breath caught in her throat as he peeled the cover

back enough to expose the twin peaks of her breasts, his hands cupping and shaping the engorged flesh and his thumbs teasing her nipples into hard life even as his mouth took her gasps.

'I want to eat you alive.' His voice was a husky growl. 'Do you know that? Devour you…'

She had missed him so much. Even as the thought took shape a polite knock sounded on the bedroom door. 'Hannah.' With a sound deep in his throat, which could have been a groan or a sigh, Taylor straightened up, moving the cover up to her neck as she just stared at him dazedly. 'You were supposed to be drinking that—' he indicated a now cold cup of tea on the table at the side of the bed '—while she prepared your breakfast.'

As the knock came again, he said, 'Okay if she comes in?' brushing back a lock of her hair which had tumbled across her face as he spoke.

'Of course.' She jerked her head away from him, humiliation and self-contempt making her voice sharp. He clicked his fingers and she came to heel like an obedient puppy—was that what he was thinking? Why on earth had she allowed him to kiss her like that, caress and touch her? Why hadn't she resisted more forcefully?

His eyes narrowed slightly at the tone of her voice, but other than that he gave no sign that he was aware of her discomfiture, merely rising from the bed before he called for Hannah to enter.

Hannah fussed and babied her as she plumped the pillows for her patient and settled the tray on the invalid's lap, but Marsha didn't mind the other woman's attention. Hannah had been widowed in her native Jamaica after only fifteen months of marriage, the shock of her husband's death through drowning, when his fishing boat had been sunk in a storm, bringing on the birth of their first child over two months early. The baby, a little girl, had lived for an hour, and had been buried in her father's arms.

Hannah had told her the story one afternoon, shortly after Marsha had got engaged to Taylor, adding that for a long time afterwards she had—in her own words—gone a little crazy. Then, due to her youngest sister marrying a rich American, Hannah had been given the chance to move to the United States and take up residence in her brother-in-law's home when his housekeeper had walked out after a row with the new wife.

It had been a way of escape from the downward spiral of depression and increasingly strong medication, and Hannah had taken it, only to find she could fully sympathise with the previous housekeeper when she had worked for her sister for a little while. But she had stuck with the only chance she'd had of making a new life, and in due course, when the husband had entertained Taylor for a few days—the two men having met through a business deal years earlier and consequently become friends—had got to know the young Englishman.

When Taylor had offered her employment in England—with the blessing of her brother-in-law, who was getting increasingly irritated by the two sisters' altercations—Hannah had accepted on the spot, and the rest, as Hannah had said, was history. And whilst Taylor strongly objected to any attempts of Hannah to mother him, Marsha had instantly recognised the need the other woman hid beneath her bustling exterior. The housekeeper was the sort of woman who should have had a houseful of children to keep her busy, and as the affection between the older and younger woman had grown Hannah had made no bones about the fact that she was longing for the day when the patter of tiny feet would occur.

Once they were alone again, Taylor raised wry eyebrows at Marsha. 'She's as pleased as punch you're here.'

Marsha said nothing. She was half sitting up in bed, with the tray balanced on her lap and the duvet wrapped round her. She needed the loo, and she wanted to put something on before she ate, neither of which could be sorted until Taylor left.

If nothing else, Taylor was intuitive. 'You would prefer me to leave you in peace?' he said easily, apparently not in the least put out.

'Yes, please.' She was not about to mince words.

'Pity.' The tawny eyes touched her lips for a second, causing her flesh to tingle. 'You used to enjoy breakfast in bed with me.'

Memories of those times, when the coffee had invariably got cold along with the food whilst they'd indulged in a different sort of nourishment, brought the heat to her cheeks, but she managed a brittle smile. 'You've already eaten,' she pointed out evenly, 'and those times are in the past.'

'True.' He let his gaze sweep over her again. 'But only for the moment.'

'I don't think so, Taylor.'

'I know so.' His smile was confident and infuriating. 'We are man and wife, and I'm damned if I'll let some sick bozo smash everything. I was hoping you'd come to see the truth for yourself, but that was asking too much. No matter.' He moved closer to the bed, leaning over her with one hand on the headboard. 'You've proved you are more than capable of surviving without me, Fuzz. Okay? Now you can choose to be with me because you want to be. And you do want me, like I want you.'

He bent down, and she gave herself over to his kiss even as she berated herself for flirting with the danger of becoming vulnerable.

It only lasted for a few moments before he straightened, his voice cool as he said, 'Now, eat your breakfast, like a good wife, and put any thought of going into work out of your head. We are spending the day together, all right? I've put a very lucrative business deal on ice because of you, not to mention a couple of meetings and a discussion with my accountant.'

'Am I supposed to be grateful?' She eyed him hotly.

He smiled again and reached for her left hand, raising it to his lips as he kissed her ringless third finger. 'You might have discarded the visible evidence of our union, but you can't discard what is in here—' he touched the area over his heart '—so easily, my love. I know you. You're in every nerve and sinew, every breath.'

She snatched her hand back, her cheeks fiery. 'Then you should know I'm not the type of woman to accept adultery as part of the marriage contract,' she bit out furiously.

'I would never have married you if you were.'

Marsha stared at him. There was no mockery and no hesitation in his voice, and the questions which had risen to the surface after Nicki had expressed her doubts over the validity of what Susan had told her flooded in again.

Her fingers tightened briefly on the tray before she told herself not to be so silly. Susan had no reason to lie, not one. And Tanya was beautiful. Beautiful and clever and— And *married*? But that didn't mean anything. Taylor's secretary had not been married at the time she had been told of their affair; that was the point she had to concentrate on here.

'I'll make you eat every word of accusation, Fuzz. I promise you that.' There was darkness in his face now, and for a moment she felt a dart of fear. 'But that's nothing to what I'll do to the person who fed you such garbage. The mind games stop today, do you hear me?'

'Mind games?' She didn't have a clue what he was talking about.

He held her gaze for ever, until finally his square jaw released its tight clench. 'Eat your breakfast,' he said silkily. 'We'll talk later.'

And he turned and left the room.

Once Marsha had visited the *en suite* bathroom, pulling on one of the guest robes hanging on the back of the door before she left the gleaming marble surrounds, she found to her absolute amazement she was ravenous.

She demolished the plateful of eggs, bacon and sausages, the two slices of toast and blackcurrant preserve and the pot of coffee the breakfast tray held in indecent haste, before sinking back against the bedhead and staring straight ahead.

A bath. She nodded at the thought, refusing to think of Taylor until she was clean and groomed again. The tiny shower room in her bedsit was all very well, but a long warm scented bath would be sheer heaven, and if ever she had needed a touch of heavenly comfort it was now.

It was five minutes later, when she was engulfed in a sea of perfumed bubbles and trying to empty her mind of everything but the pleasure her body was experiencing, that she suddenly sat up with enough force to send water slopping over the side of the bath. Why hadn't

Taylor placed her in *their* bed last night? She had been out of it, she admitted, and hardly in a position to resist any overtures on his part, so why hadn't he taken advantage of the situation? Not that he would have forced himself on her when she was unwell, she didn't think that for a moment, but if she had been in their bed then this morning would have been a different kettle of fish entirely. To wake up beside him...

She sank down again, a frown crinkling her brow as she pondered the thought. When she had left him she had left practically every article of clothing and every personal item she possessed, and from what he had intimated this morning her clothes, at least, were still all in place. He could have used that as an excuse to have her in his bed. Not that Taylor had ever needed an excuse for something he wanted to do, she reflected acidly.

She raised one foot from beneath the foam, studying her scarlet-painted toenails thoughtfully. If they had woken up together the inevitable would have happened; he must know that. She had never been able to resist him, and he was fully aware of his sexual power.

Another half an hour of rumination brought her no nearer to an answer other than the obvious one—he hadn't wanted her to share their room again. As she rose from the now cool water she refused to let the idea hurt. They would no longer be married in a few weeks' time, and once she left this house today she would make sure she never set foot in it again. She didn't understand Taylor Kane, she had *never* understood him, and she wasn't about to waste any more time trying.

She flexed shoulders which should have been relaxed after the amount of time she had been lying in the water but were taut and tense, and then proceeded to dry herself with a big fluffy towel. It was as she was smoothing scented body lotion on every inch of skin that she stopped suddenly, gazing into the mirror in front of her. She needed to talk to Susan. Her heart began to thud as she accepted the notion which had been hammering away at the door of her mind ever since Nicki had expressed her doubts about the other woman's motives.

A sound from the room outside, and then a knock on the *en suite* door jerked her out of her musing. She whipped the bath towel round her, folding a smaller one turban-style round her wet hair, before padding across and opening the door.

'Hi.' Taylor smiled at her. 'I was beginning to think you'd drowned in there.'

'It was nice to have a bath for a change.' And at his raised eyebrows she explained, 'I only have a shower at home.'

There was a quick, almost imperceptible change in his expression. 'This is your home.'

Marsha brushed past him, ignoring the swift reaction of her body to his nearness. She paused in the middle of the bedroom, turning to face him as she said, 'Are my clothes ready now?'

'No.' He offered no more explanation before he said, 'But, like I said earlier, you have a wardrobe full of things in our room. Come and select what you want to wear.'

She stiffened. It was bad enough being in her old home in one of the guest rooms; she didn't know how she would handle entering the room where they had enjoyed so many hours of love and tenderness and passion. But she couldn't let him see that. He would regard it as weakness and play on it accordingly. 'Fine.' She raised her chin and aimed a level stare.

Taylor's mouth twitched. 'Personally, I think you look great in what you're wearing now,' he said easily, his eyes going to her head. 'Sort of...eastern, harem-like.'

Marsha ground her teeth at the implication. No doubt he would just love to have his own little bevy of beauties dancing at his beck and call, but she was blowed if she'd be one of them. 'I hardly think a handtowel wrapped round one's head deserves such a comment,' she said coolly.

'Perhaps not.' He tilted his head, and now the amusement crept into his eyes. 'But a man can dream, can't he?'

She had no intention of continuing down this path, and she wished she had taken the time to put the towelling robe back on when he had knocked. It was infinitely more reassuring than a towel. Battling a number of emotions, none of which were clear, she said, 'My clothes?'

'Of course.' He turned, opening the bedroom door and then bowing slightly. 'When you're ready, ma'am.'

Even though she had prepared herself for the moment when Taylor opened the door to their bedroom, Marsha felt something akin to an electric shock travel down each nerve-end as she entered the big spacious room. The windows had been flung wide open, and the scent of lavender from the grounds below was sweet. Her eyes were drawn to the huge bed which dominated the cream and coffee-coloured room, but she forced herself to remain blank-faced as she marched across to her walk-in wardrobe.

Everything was just as she had left it, she noticed, down to the last pair of shoes on the racks below her clothes—and the perfume she had worn during her marriage—a madly expensive extravagance first bought on honeymoon—still lingered in the air.

She swallowed hard, keeping her back to the room as she selected a light pair of trousers and a short-sleeved top, along with a bra and pair of panties. There were several pairs of sandals at one end of the wardrobe, and she chose a low-heeled style suitable for a working day. She still intended to go into work that afternoon, but she wasn't about to announce it again until she was ready to leave.

'Thank you.' After closing the wardrobe door she nodded at Taylor, who was leaning against the far wall, strong muscled arms crossed over his chest and a faintly brooding expression on his face. 'I'll see you downstairs, shall I?'

'What do you feel? Coming in here again, I mean.'

'What?' He had taken her completely by surprise. Her eyes flickered with momentary panic, quickly controlled. She shrugged carefully. 'It's a beautiful room,' she said steadily.

'That's not what I asked,' he countered coolly.

'How do you think I feel?' She found herself glaring at him now and warned herself to tread warily. No show of emotion, no challenges. 'A little sad, I guess,' she added quickly.

'A little sad?' Something flashed in his eyes at her words. 'A little sad as in having your guts torn out by their roots, or the sort of feeling you would have when watching a weepy movie?'

'Taylor, I don't want to do this.'

'Tough.' He took a step nearer and instinctively she brought the clothes up to her chest. 'We've done it your way all through this and where have we got?' His eyes locked on hers, anchoring her to the spot. 'I want to know what you are thinking for once, damn it. All through our marriage—right from when we met, in fact—I've had to pull what you're thinking out of you like a dentist extracting a tooth. I'm sick of it.'

She stared at him, her eyes hot as her temper rose. 'I didn't ask you to bring me here,' she shot at him furiously, 'and if you're so sick of me, wouldn't it be best for both of us if I left right now?'

'As always, you don't hear what I'm saying.' He reached her in one fluid movement, gripping her shoulders as he said, 'I'm sick of the lack of communication, not you. There's a difference there, if you'd open your eyes to see it. I never wanted a clinging vine who couldn't say boo to a goose and lived in my shadow, but you're something else. It's like there's an invisible wall round you, and however high I climb I never get to the top. You've never really let me in, have you? Not in all the months we were together did I ever feel I'd breached the guard you keep round the real you.'

'And that's why you slept with Tanya?' she flung at him bitterly. 'Because I didn't fall at your feet and worship you like all the others?'

'Give me strength! Listen, woman, will you? This is about me and you, not Tanya or anyone else. From the day I met you I've never looked at another woman. You're enough—more than enough,' he added scathingly, 'for any man to handle.'

'I don't believe you.'

'No, and do you know why you accepted those lies about me and our marriage so easily? Because you are frightened of the truth.'

'You're crazy,' she said harshly, aware she would have bruises where his hands were gripping her.

'About you? I must be, to put up with all this stuff

and nonsense. You are petrified of letting go and giving me everything. That's the crux of all this. If you trust me absolutely I'll let you down—that's what you've told yourself from day one. And then, surprise, surprise, you were told exactly what you were waiting to hear—I'd fallen from grace. I was having an affair. It must have been music to your ears.'

'That's a hateful thing to say.'

'But this is Taylor talking, remember? The low-life, the scum who was fooling around just eighteen months after he had promised to forsake all others for the rest of his life.'

'You're hurting me.' She was rigid and as white as a sheet under his hands.

'Damn it, Marsha.' His muttered oath had all the power of a shout, and she almost winced before she controlled herself. But he had released her.

He stepped backwards a pace or two, as though he didn't trust himself not to take hold of her again, and then, slowly and deliberately, he slipped his hands into his pockets. 'You still believe, without a shadow of a doubt, that I'm guilty as charged?' he asked in a flat grim tone which frightened her far more than his rage.

Did she? The answer was there without her having to think about it, and she spoke it out without considering her words. 'I don't know what to think any more. I was sure…' She hesitated. 'I mean, why would anyone make something like that up?'

He shook his head, his eyes mordant. 'How long have you got? Come on, Fuzz, you can't pretend to be that naive. There's a hundred reasons why people turn sour.'

But it was your sister. Your *sister*. For a second she thought she had actually spoken the words out loud, but when his expression didn't alter she knew the shout had just been in her mind.

'I hoped when you'd had time to think about all this you would begin to question—at least that. If you couldn't trust me, surely that wasn't too much to ask, was it? But there was just silence. No contact, no phone calls, no answer to my letter. So I told myself to be patient, to wait. We loved each other and no one could take that away. Hell!' It was bitter. 'And I called *you* naive.'

Marsha stared at him for a moment before turning her head aside. She had the terrible feeling deep inside that everything had shifted again. Just when she had trained herself to get through each twenty-four hours without him he was back in her life, turning over all the stones to examine the dirt beneath. And she didn't want to do that. It had nearly killed her, leaving him, but she had managed to crawl through the weeks and months since, and that was something.

She shut her eyes, her hands clenching into fists at her sides. 'Why are you doing this?'

'Because someone has to. You would actually throw away everything we had without fighting for it. I realise that now. So it's up to me to fight for both of us. Who was it? Who talked to you?'

'I…I can't say. I promised.'

He swore, a savage oath. 'You promised me more. Remember? Love, honour, cherish, in sickness and in health? You owe me a name, damn it.'

'Taylor, I—'

'A name, Marsha. Then maybe we can start to get to the bottom of this. If I'd had my head screwed on I'd have done this months ago, instead of assuming you could actually reason like any sane human being.'

It opened her eyes and brought her head up. She was so angry she wanted to stamp and scream like a child. He was intent on blaming everything on her, even when the evidence against him had been stacked to the sky. He would never know how much she had suffered when she had made that call to the hotel and heard Tanya speak in her sexy little-girl voice from their room. 'You don't want to know who it was,' she said tightly. 'Take it from me.'

'I do.' His eyes were boring into her and his face was harder than she had ever seen it, unreachable.

She stared at him, Susan's name hovering on her tongue even as her mind raced. If she told Taylor his sister had betrayed him, what would it do to his and Susan's relationship? Smash it for ever. He was not the sort of man to forgive; she knew that. Whether Susan's accusation was true or not, he would cut her out of his life with the ruthlessness that had got him to where he was now. And that would mean Dale, her husband, would lose his job, perhaps even their house, because no one would pay Dale what Taylor paid him.

Of course if Susan had lied she deserved all that and maybe more—but if she hadn't...? And Taylor? What would it do to him? He loved his sister; she was all the natural family he had. Oh, what should she do? She was in a no-win situation here and so was he, if he did but know it. Tough as he was, his sister occupied a very special place in his heart, as he did in Susan's. That was what made this whole thing so impossible. Susan *had* to have been telling the truth...didn't she?

'I'm sorry, Taylor.' She kept her eyes steady despite the growing darkness in his face.

'I see.'

No—no, he didn't see, but what could she do? She

The Reader Service™ — Here's how it works:

Accepting the free books places you under no obligation to buy anything. You may keep the books and gift and return the despatch note marked 'cancel'. If we do not hear from you, about a month later we'll send you 6 brand new books and invoice you just £2.69* each. That's the complete price - there is no extra charge for postage and packing. You may cancel at any time, otherwise every month we'll send you 6 more books, which you may either purchase or return to us - the choice is yours.

*Terms and prices subject to change without notice.

THE READER SERVICE™
FREE BOOK OFFER
FREEPOST CN81
CROYDON
CR9 3WZ

NO STAMP
NECESSARY
IF POSTED IN
THE U.K. OR N.I.

would have to go and see Susan as soon as possible. Maybe talking to her would settle some things. 'I...I can't tell you. I would if there was a way, but—'

'Forget it.' His tone was final and very cold.

'Forget it?' Her mouth had opened in a little O of surprise.

'Go and get dressed, Marsha.' He stood aside, his face closed against her.

In spite of herself she reached out her hand, touching his broad chest in a helpless little gesture that carried a wealth of pleading in it. He didn't move a muscle, merely watching her with narrowed amber eyes that were as cool and unemotional as the resin they resembled.

When her hand fell back to her side she turned swiftly and walked across the room without looking at him again, making her way to the guest room on legs that trembled. Once inside she locked the door, her eyes burning with unshed tears and the lump in her throat threatening to choke her. It was over. The look in his eyes had told her so.

She walked across to the bed and sank down on it, still holding the clothes in her hands. He didn't want her any more. He had said he was sick of her and the last minute or two had proved it. She ought to be pleased.

She pressed a hand to her mouth, the tears falling hot and fast as she rocked to and fro in an agony of grief, feeling more desolate than she had ever felt before.

Five minutes later and she had pulled herself together sufficiently to pick up the telephone and request a taxi-cab. After washing her face she dressed quickly, running a comb through her hair and applying some lipstick—the only item of make-up she had with her.

She couldn't countenance an afternoon in Taylor's company; she felt too raw. Okay, it might look as if she was running away—and maybe she was, she admitted wretchedly—but this was pure self-survival. Reaching for her handbag, she extracted a little notebook and scribbled a quick message to Hannah, promising the older woman she would ring her soon and arrange for them to meet up somewhere. Then, feeling like someone in a bad drama on TV, she crept carefully downstairs and out of the front door, hurrying down the drive.

She was so relieved to see the taxi waiting just beyond the entrance to the drive she could have kissed the small balding man behind the wheel. Instead she clambered in quickly, giving him the address of the bedsit and then changing her mind in the next instant and telling him to take her straight into work. If Taylor came after her—and it was a big if, considering how they had parted—she would rather have the security of a work environment than be all alone at the bedsit.

She didn't begin to breathe freely until they were well on their way, and right until she actually walked into the building she felt as though at any moment a hand would tap her on the shoulder or a deep unmistakable voice would call her name. But then she was in the lift, being transported to her floor, and she knew she had done it.

And, strangely, in that moment she felt more miserable than ever.

CHAPTER SIX

'WHEN do you think he'll realise the bird has flown the nest?'

Nicki placed a steaming mug of coffee in front of her as she spoke, and Marsha took a careful sip of the scalding liquid before she said, 'He must know by now.'

'Worried?'

'No.' Marsha's fingers tightened on the mug. 'Why should I be? He doesn't own me, and I'm blowed if I'll let him tell me whether I can come into work or not.'

'Good on you.' Nicki was all approval. 'He ought to be crawling on his hands and knees begging forgiveness for the way he's treated you.'

Marsha looked up from the coffee, her eyes narrowing. She might be wrong, but hadn't Nicki changed tack somewhat from yesterday? Then she had been urging her to give Taylor the benefit of the doubt. Now she sounded as if she'd like to punch him on the nose. 'What have you heard?' she asked flatly.

'Heard?' Nicki flushed a deep pink as she sat down at her own desk, fiddling unnecessarily with some papers as she said, 'What makes you think I've heard something?'

Marsha didn't bother to reply, merely raising her eyebrows and lowering her chin while she waited for the other woman to look up.

There was a pause before Nicki glanced at her. 'It's just something Janie said, that's all.'

'Which was?'

Nicki wriggled uncomfortably. 'Penelope has swung the contract for Kane International and he—your husband—is taking her out for a meal to celebrate.'

Marsha shrugged. 'It's a free country,' she said, as lightly as she could.

'Dinner at the Hot Spot.'

Marsha took a moment to steady her voice. 'We're separated, Nicki. He's allowed to see anyone he wants.' The Hot Spot was the latest big sensation with London's jet set: a nightclub where you could dance the night away and even get breakfast in the morning. No one went there just for dinner.

Nicki sniffed a very eloquent sniff. 'I've never liked tall dark men,' she said flatly. 'Especially when their egos match their…hat size.'

'I've never seen Taylor in a hat.'

The two women stared at each other for a moment before they both smiled weakly. 'I'll get you a sandwich while you get stuck into that report,' Nicki said quietly.

'Thanks.'

The rest of the day passed without incident. Nicki insisted Marsha have dinner with herself and her husband, and after a pleasant evening in their Paddington flat they drove her home, waiting outside until she waved to them from the bedsit window to say all was well. Their concern was sweet, but made Marsha feel slightly ridiculous. Taylor wasn't violent, for goodness' sake, or dangerous—not in an abusive sense anyway. She knew he would rather cut off his right hand than raise it to a woman. She very much doubted his pride would allow him to try and see her again anyway, outside of the divorce court.

She slept badly that night, tossing and turning and drifting into one nightmare after another until, at just gone six, she rose from her rumpled bed and had a long warm shower. Thank goodness it was Friday and she had the weekend in front of her to get a handle on all this. She needed to be able to take a long walk in the fresh air and get her thoughts in order.

She always thought better out in the open. It was a hangover from her childhood and teenage years, when she had liked nothing better than to escape the confines of the dormitory and communal dining hall and wander about in the grounds of the home, staying out until she was found and brought back by an irate assistant.

It was during those times that she had eventually come to terms with the fact that it was probably her fault she had been returned to the home twice when adoption attempts had fallen through.

She had told herself so often the story of how her mother would come back for her—arms open wide as she tearfully told her daughter how much she loved her—that she had been unable to separate fact from fiction. She couldn't not be there when her mother came, she had determined, and so—much as she hated it—she couldn't live anywhere else.

It was after her best friend had left the home and forgotten all her extravagant promises to write and visit that she had begun to face the prospect that just wishing for people to behave a certain way didn't mean it was going to happen. But by then it had been too late.

She had been labelled withdrawn and difficult, and was no longer a cute little girl, but a gawky youngster approaching teenage years with braces on her teeth and spots on her chin.

By the time the ugly duckling had turned into a diffident and shy swan she had learnt she could rely on no one but herself. If she didn't expect anything of anyone she wouldn't be disappointed, and if she didn't let anyone get near they wouldn't be able to hurt her. Simple.

Only it hadn't worked that way with Taylor. From the second she had seen him she had wanted him; it had been as clear and unequivocal as that. Not that she hadn't known it was madness.

She turned off the shower, wrapping a towel round her and walking through into the main room. Sunlight was already slanting golden shafts into the room and the day promised to be another warm one.

Yes, she'd known it was madness, she reiterated as she dried her hair. Deep inside she'd continually asked herself how serious he was about relinquishing his love 'em and leave 'em lifestyle. Did he want her for a lifetime? Did he need her as she needed him? Could she handle the complex being that was Taylor Kane? Would he grow bored with marriage or, worse, her? Those questions had plagued her from day one.

'Who fed your insecurities with the very thing you most feared?' Taylor's words came back to her with piercing suddenness, causing her hand to still before she threw the hairdryer on to the sofa.

He had insisted on his innocence that night eighteen months ago and he was still insisting on it. Had he sent her a letter giving the telephone number of this stranger who had allowed him to share his room in Germany? It was easy for him to say so now, when so much time had elapsed, and surely it was more than a little far-fetched to think the letter had got lost in the post?

The ring of the telephone right at her elbow made her jump a mile, and she put a hand to her racing heart before glancing at her watch. Six-thirty. Who on earth was calling her at six-thirty?

She refused to admit she was expecting it to be

Taylor, but the minute she lifted the receiver and heard his voice her heart galloped even faster. He had spoken only her name, his voice even, and she couldn't tell what sort of mood he was in.

'Hello, Taylor.' She was pleased to hear her voice betrayed nothing of what she was feeling.

'Did I wake you?'

Prevarication seemed the best response. She wasn't about to let him know she had been up with the birds because he had invaded her dreams as well as every waking moment. 'It *is* six-thirty in the morning,' she said coolly. 'I don't normally rise before seven.' Which was true.

'I couldn't sleep.' His voice was warm and soft and did the craziest things to her nerve-endings.

Marsha breathed out very slowly. 'Most people reach for a book rather than the phone in that situation.'

'I'm not most people.'

Now, that was definitely the truest thing he had ever said! She stared at the painted wall some feet away, trying to work out where he was coming from. He didn't sound mad, but he had always been able to conceal anger very well. 'What do you want?' she asked carefully.

'You.' It was immediate. 'But I'll settle for breakfast.'

In his dreams! She forced a sarcastic laugh. 'I don't think so.'

'No?'

'No.'

'Oh, well, I guess I can throw stones at Mrs Tate-Collins's window and see if she's in the mood for warm croissants. Say what you like, but I think I might be in with a chance there.'

She stared at the receiver as she tried to assimilate the implication of what he had just said. 'Where are you, exactly?' she said flatly.

'Exactly?' The pause was deliberate. 'Well, if we're talking exactly, I'm on the second paving slab to the left of the steps which lead up to the front door of your building.'

He was *outside*? For a second she was tempted to tell him to go ahead and wake Mrs Tate-Collins, but knowing he would almost certainly call her bluff restrained her. She didn't want him sitting in the basement telling Mrs Tate-Collins all the ins and outs of this ridiculous situation, as he knew full well.

She tried one last time. 'Go home, Taylor.'

'No chance.'

She dipped her head, shaking it irritably before she said, 'Doesn't what I want count for anything?'

'Absolutely not. We've done it your way over the last months and what have we got? No nearer to sorting anything out and even more tangles in the web.'

'I could get a restraining order. That way you wouldn't be able to keep harassing me.'

'You could try.' It was mordant. 'But I doubt if any court in the land would agree that offering you dinner, giving you a helping hand when you were sick and then calling by with breakfast constitutes harassment.'

She took a deep breath to combat the anger his supremely confident voice had aroused. He took the biscuit for sheer arrogance. 'I'll open the front door.'

'Thanks.'

Sixty seconds later a light knock announced his arrival. She had just had time to pull on a pair of cream cotton combat trousers and a sleeveless top, but with her newly washed hair shining like raw silk and her skin fresh and clean from the shower she felt more than able to hold her own. She didn't rush to answer the door, waiting for a moment or two before she pulled it open.

Taylor was standing with a box in his arms, his smile lazy and his amber eyes reflecting the golden sunlight from the landing window. 'Good morning.' He waited for an invitation to enter.

She inclined her head, refusing to let him see what his presence did to her. He was wearing black jeans and an open-necked black denim shirt and he looked magnificent. 'Come in,' she said grudgingly.

He quirked a brow at her tone but said nothing, walking past her and then standing just inside the room. 'This is great.' He couldn't quite disguise his surprise.

'I like it.' She had opened the balcony windows first thing, and now he walked across the room, after depositing the box on the breakfast bar, standing and looking out over the rooftops for a moment or two.

Turning, he said, 'Did you have to do much when you first moved in?'

'Quite a bit.' It felt very strange, having him stand in her little home, and to cover her agitation she began to unpack the box of food he had brought as she detailed her additions and alterations to the bedsit.

He had brought warm croissants, as he had said, along with a selection of preserves in tiny individual jars, and cold cooked meats, cheese, hard-boiled eggs and potato salad. Melon, kiwi, grapefruit, mango and other fruits—all ready prepared and sliced in containers—along with a variety of cereals and fresh orange juice made up the box, at the top of which lay a deep red rose, its petals still damp with the morning dew.

Marsha made no comment about the rose, placing it to one side. It seemed safer.

'Do you really mind me bringing breakfast round?'

He had come up behind her, his breath warm on the back of her neck. She was not fooled by the gentle persuasive tone. He was using the Kane charm, and it could be lethal on occasion. 'Actually, yes.' She used the excuse of fetching plates and bowls to put a few feet between them.

'Why?'

She turned, her hands full, and found herself facing his chest. He had moved as lightly and swiftly as a cat. 'Because this is my home and I prefer to invite callers.' As he made a move to take the crockery from her she said, 'I can manage, thank you.'

'I'm sure you can.' He took it, nevertheless, setting it down on the breakfast bar and then perching on one of the stools which he had pulled out further into the room. 'But there's more to life than managing, surely?'

She warned herself not to get drawn into this. 'You know what I meant.'

'And you know what I meant. I've existed, not lived, the last eighteen months. Tell me you haven't done the same.' He raked back his hair as he spoke and the simple action created a surge of sexual need inside her she couldn't believe.

'I've been fine. I *am* fine.' She stared straight at him, refusing to blink as she lied.

'You're getting better at lying, but you'll never really master the art,' he said comfortably.

'I see the giant ego is still alive and healthy.'

'However, I would say you've improved beyond measure with the putdowns.'

He had an answer for everything, impossible man. She had promised herself she wouldn't show any emotion, but now her green eyes glowed like an angry cat's as she glared at him. 'You're the only person who ever affects me that way,' she said, without thinking about her words.

She saw the tawny gaze widen for a second and realised what she had said. 'No one else is as rude or pushy as you,' she qualified quickly.

He stared at her, his expression carefully masked but with a slight smile playing at the corners of his mouth which was more annoying than any challenge. 'Relax, Fuzz. I'm not about to leap on you and have my wicked way. This is just breakfast, okay?'

Too true it was. Did he really think she would just fall into his arms like a ripe plum if he made a move? She raised her chin. 'I didn't expect to hear from you again after the way I left the house.'

'Yes, you did,' he argued softly. 'You knew I wouldn't be able to keep away from you.'

'You managed it fairly successfully for eighteen months.' She had intended her words to be barbed, but they merely sounded faintly woebegone.

'I've told you why. You needed to face certain issues and work them through so you could see the truth for yourself and make the first move to reconciliation.'

'Well, that didn't work, did it?'

He smiled. 'I do occasionally get it wrong. That ought to please you.'

She shrugged, picking up one of the fruit containers, only to have it taken out of her hand in the next moment. 'Look at me, Fuzz,' he said quietly, his voice gentle. 'I mean *really* look at me. Can't you see I've been in hell the last months? Don't you know I've been half crazy?'

As he spoke, he stroked the back of his fingers across

her cheek, his other arm enclosing her into the warmth of him. 'Don't.' It was feeble and they both knew it.

'The touch, the feel, the smell of you.' His voice was even softer, the amber eyes mesmerising. 'I've thought of nothing else. When you were in that wretched little bed and breakfast I used to come and park a few doors away late at night, just so I could be in the same vicinity as you. How's that for crazy? And then when you moved here if I picked up the phone once to call, I did it a thousand times.'

'Why didn't you follow through?' she asked weakly.

'I thought I was doing the best for us, for our future. Those gremlins that dog you have got to be brought into the light and destroyed. Oh, Fuzz...' He took her mouth in the gentlest of kisses, his tenderness beguiling her utterly. 'You're perfect, don't you know that? Everything I could ever want.'

This time when his mouth fastened on hers the pressure was more intense, and now both arms held her to him. He was kissing her in the way she remembered, a way which made her body ache for him. His hands roamed up and down the silky skin of her arms before moving one strap of her top aside so his lips could caress the smooth flesh of her shoulder. She shivered and his attentions increased. Her arms instinctively lifted as he raised the bottom of the top and pulled it over her head.

'Beautiful...' It was a throaty murmur as his hands cupped and moulded the full mounds of her breasts, his thumbs playing over the hard peaks of her nipples. 'Ravishingly beautiful.'

When his mouth took what his hands had just admired, she couldn't help arching back, a moan escaping her lips as hot sensation curled like electricity from the tip of her left breast right into the core of her. She dug her fingers into his shoulders, her legs trembling so much she couldn't hide how deeply he was affecting her.

When his hands moved to the clip on her trousers she was beyond protest. His own clothes followed hers a moment later until they were both naked, their skin warm and moist. She inhaled the clean smell of his lemony aftershave, its sharp tang mixed with his own musky scent to produce an erotic perfume that was pure Taylor. She had so missed him... It was the only thought she was capable of.

There was a fire inside her as he explored her mouth and body with a slow, pleasure-inducing enjoyment which brought them both to the peak of arousal. And she touched him, running her fingers over the hard-muscled lines of his powerful body, across the broad, hair-roughened chest and the solid bridge of his shoulders.

There was an infinite hunger inside her which only the feel of him deep in her innermost being could assuage, and when at last he thrust into her molten body her muscles contracted to hold him tight in the silken sheath. She was leaning against the smooth cool wall now, but then he raised her with his hands on her bottom, forcing her long legs to wrap themselves around his hips as their bodies entwined still closer.

When the release came its explosion took them both into a shattering world of light and colour and sensation in which time had no meaning. There was no past and no future, and even the present consisted only of the swirling heights to which they had risen. Passion was the master, and it was all the more powerful for being denied so long.

Her head was resting against the hard column of his throat as he cradled her against him, the furious pounding of his heart beginning to diminish as he placed small burning kisses on her brow.

It wasn't until he gently lowered her feet to the floor that she began to think again, but even then she was so wrapped up in his arms as he continued to hold her close against him that the full import didn't register. 'I love you, sweetheart.' His voice was muffled above her head but warm with lingering passion. 'Never doubt that for a moment.'

She continued to rest against the lean bulk of him, but now reality wouldn't be kept at bay. She had allowed Taylor to make love to her. No, not just allowed it—encouraged it, begged for it, she admitted silently, feeling numb with shame.

'This is where you say you love me too.'

The beginning of her reply was lost in his kiss as he bent his head, but after a moment or two the lack of response must have got through to him. He raised his head, his eyes taking in her mortified face. 'We're married, Fuzz,' he reminded her evenly. 'It's okay to say you love me.'

He was saying it was okay for much more than that, and they both knew it. 'We—we're separated,' she protested faintly.

He held her away from him for a second, his gaze conducting a leisurely evaluation of the space between them. 'So we are,' he agreed lazily, his voice deep with throaty amusement. 'But I can soon remedy that again, if you so wish?'

In spite of herself her body tingled where his eyes had stroked, and now her face was scarlet. For months she had been fiercely telling herself that she was able to make a new life in which Taylor played no part. She was a career woman now; she was going to concentrate on that and that alone. Men, romance, sex—she didn't want any of it. There were too many complications, too many compromises, too much heartache. And what had happened to all her grand thoughts and principles? Taylor had happened. He had crooked his little finger after eighteen months of silence and she had flown into his arms like a homing pigeon. It was her worst nightmare come to life.

'We shouldn't have done this.' She pulled herself free, yanking the throw off the sofa and wrapping it round her. 'It will only complicate things.'

'I doubt they could get more complicated,' he said mildly.

'Of course they can.'

He didn't contradict her this time. He simply stood there, stark naked and faintly amused as he surveyed her frantic face. After a moment he said, very calmly, 'I don't know about you but I'm starving. Shall we eat?'

Shall we eat? She stared at him, her cheeks pink and her hair ruffled. Men were a different species, they really were.

'Fuzz, you haven't done anything wrong.' It was said in tones of insulting patience, the sort of voice one used with a child who was being particularly silly. 'We've just enjoyed one of the most natural pleasures known to man—and woman.' She went even pinker, as he had meant her to. 'Besides which we *are* man and wife, for crying out loud. Or had that little fact slipped your mind with it being so long?'

Nothing about Taylor had ever slipped her mind. 'The...the divorce.' Had he made love to her just to put a spanner in the works? She wouldn't put it past him.

She wouldn't put *anything* past him. 'Will it make a difference if the solicitors find out?'

'I tell you what, I won't tell if you don't.' His face had closed against her as she had spoken, and now he bent to retrieve his clothes, beginning to dress with lazy grace.

She watched him miserably, more confused than she had ever been in her life. She loved him. She had never stopped loving him even when she had told herself she hated him for what he had done. But did she trust him? Did she really believe he had just been Tanya's boss and that was all? Did she know, deep in her heart, that there had never been any other women since he had met her? The answer sent a bleak chill through her, quelling any words of appeasement.

Once he was dressed he looked at her, no expression on his face now. 'I can't carry you kicking and screaming out of that place of shadows you inhabit and into the real world,' he said quietly. 'And I can't show you any more clearly how I feel. You're destroying us—you know that, don't you? Throwing away something which should have lasted for a lifetime and beyond. I know what your mother did was tough, along with the rest of it, but sooner or later you have to make up your mind whether anything at all is worth fighting for. If it is, we should be at the top of the list.'

'I didn't ask you to come here this morning,' she said numbly.

'No, you didn't.' He nodded his agreement. 'But I came anyway, so that should tell you something. And don't say it was because of what we've just done either. If it was just sex I wanted there are any number of women I could call on. That's the way of it when you are wealthy and successful. I don't want sex, Fuzz. I want to make love. With you. There's a hell of a difference there. Do you see that?'

She stared at him, her eyes huge. 'I don't know what to think any more. I'm—'

'Confused.' Taylor confirmed his understanding with a nod. 'But not knowing what to think is better than being sure of the wrong thing. Maybe there's hope for you yet.'

She couldn't return his smile. She felt raw and exposed and his last words had done nothing to calm her agitation. Taylor was the master of manipulation. Had this morning been an exercise in psyching her out? If so it had been an extremely rewarding one as far as he was concerned.

'Get dressed, Fuzz.' His smile was replaced by a sombre gaze. 'And I promise I won't touch you again this morning, okay? We'll eat, pretend this is just the beginning of a normal working day for an old married couple.'

'I'm not hungry.' She wondered why the bedsit seemed to have shrunk since he had walked into it.

'You still need to eat.'

She wanted to argue, but she had the horrible feeling she might burst into tears if she did. Gathering up her clothes, she said, 'I'll just have a quick shower,' and scuttled across the room, closing the door of the shower room firmly behind her and then locking it. Her body felt sensuously replete, the core of her throbbing faintly with a pleasant ache and her breasts full and heavy as she showered before dressing. She eyed herself in the small mirror before leaving the tiny room and groaned softly. She had the look of a woman who had just been made love to, sure enough. She was going to have to make up very carefully once he had gone.

She took a deep breath and lifted her head, opening the shower room door and walking briskly into the main room. And then she stopped dead. It was empty. He'd gone. She glanced about her as though she expected him to leap up from behind the sofa, and then she saw the note on the breakfast bar. Walking across, she picked it up, holding the rose which he had slanted across one of the pages from the message pad she kept near the telephone.

Sorry, urgent call on my mobile means I've got to cut and run. We'll talk later. T

Marsha sank down on one of the stools, her heart thudding. T. Not even 'love T'. And surely he could have waited a few minutes until she'd showered and dressed? Had he regretted making love to her? Or had he thought it would be easier on her if he left before she came out? She had said she wasn't hungry, but—

Stop it. The command in her head was strong. No amount of rationalising would give her the answer. Only Taylor could do that, and she couldn't ask him. She put down the note and the rose, staring at the deep red petals for a long time. She had let Taylor into her mind and her body this morning; she'd gone against everything she had told herself over the last eighteen months and had given him goodness knows what message. She was stark staring mad.

Coffee. She nodded to the thought. She was going to have a cup of strong hot coffee and then force herself to eat some of this food. She would need to be fully in command of herself when she went to see Susan this morning. The time had come. Or perhaps it was long overdue. Eighteen months overdue. If nothing else she should have insisted on seeing Susan and Dale once the initial shock had subsided. She realised that now. So perhaps, as Taylor had said, there was hope for her yet? But it wasn't hope for herself she wanted, it was hope for them.

She frowned to herself, hating to admit just how much she needed him. From the moment he had come into her life, like a powerful, inexorable force, she had known she would never love anyone else. Taylor was part of her, he was in her blood, her bones, and whatever she did to try to forget him it didn't work.

It had been so good when they had first been married... She let her mind wander back to those golden days in a way she hadn't done for a long time because it was too painful. She had adored him, had been over the moon that a man like Taylor—sophisticated, handsome, wealthy, powerful—had noticed her. Not just noticed her but fallen madly in love with her if he was to be believed. And he had been so gentle, so tender with her.

She pushed back the silk of her hair, her eyes cloudy with the memories which were crowding in.

Right from their first date it had been enough to be together; they hadn't needed anyone else. In fact it had been something of a sacrifice when they had shared their time with other people, even old friends. They had practically lived in each other's pockets before they were married, their relationship so intense it had disturbed her when she stopped to think about it. Which wasn't often. Not with Taylor by her side, filling every moment, every thought, every breath.

She sighed deeply, her body still holding the tingling awareness of their lovemaking and her breasts full and heavy with the remnants of passion.

She had told him they shouldn't have made love, but it had seemed the most natural, the *right* thing to do. So where did that leave her?

Up the creek without a paddle. An old saying of the home's matron, a severe, grey-haired lady with the name of Armstrong, came to mind. Matron Armstrong had been a Yorkshire lass, and full of such little gems, but she had been kind beneath her grim exterior. Marsha could still recall when the second set of prospective parents had returned her to the home, making no effort to hide their disappointment in her, and the way Matron had whisked her into her quarters once they had gone, feeding her hot crumpets and jam by the fire and talking long and hard about how stupid some grown-ups could be. Yes, she had been a nice woman, Matron Armstrong.

She sighed again, gazing round the bedsit as though the little home she had created for herself would help her sort out her confusion. Why did she still, knowing all she knew about Tanya—or at least thought she knew, she corrected, trying to be fair—ache for his touch, his love?

Because she loved him in a way she could never love anyone else.

The thought thrust itself into the forefront of her mind, causing her to lower her head as she made a sound deep in her throat.

She sat quite still for some minutes before raising her head, and now her mouth was set in a determined line, her eyes narrowed. She would go and see Susan and bear whatever came of their meeting, good or bad. She owed it to herself to do that, even if she didn't owe it to Taylor.

CHAPTER SEVEN

SUSAN'S large, faintly ostentatious house was gently baking in the morning sun as Marsha paid the taxi driver. As he drove off she turned, standing and looking at the building for a moment.

The small select estate of three-year-old executive style properties was all manicured green lawns, pristine flower borders with not a petal in the wrong place and pocket-size back gardens without a bird in sight. Windows gleamed, drives were immaculate and the odd silver birch tree—the only trees which had been planted by the builders in the middle of every other front lawn—were neatly trimmed and perfect. Marsha found it hard to imagine that real flesh and blood people lived in such uniform perfection.

She had telephoned Susan earlier that morning, and it was clear the other woman had been keeping an eye out for the taxi as the front door suddenly opened. 'Marsha.' Susan smiled at her. 'How lovely to see you. Do come in.'

As Marsha reached her sister-in-law she was briefly enfolded in a cool perfumed embrace, and then she was in Susan's elegant cream and biscuit hall—the same colour scheme being reflected throughout the five-bedroomed house.

'Come through to the sitting room,' Susan continued, leading the way into the large and expensively furnished room Marsha remembered from when she had still been living with Taylor. Brother and sister had had a few altercations over the price of several items, not least the three two-seater cream leather sofas, the cost of which had run into six figures. Dale's salary—as Taylor's general manager—should have been able to cover the mortgage and the cost of any necessary new furniture or appliances when they had moved from their more modest house just after Marsha and Taylor had wed, but neither Susan's husband nor her brother had expected her to go on a spending spree as she had. When Susan had come crying to Taylor that she couldn't keep up the repayments on various items he had taken the debts and paid them, but not before he had made it very clear he wasn't happy with her wild squandering of what was essentially his money.

Susan had argued and cried and sulked, taking herself off for a weekend to a health farm at the height of the dispute, but with the debts all paid off and her new home furnished exactly the way she wanted she had soon been herself again—with Taylor, at least. With Dale she had seemed a little distant.

It was through this fracas that Marsha had seen Taylor's relationship with his sister was more father to daughter than sibling to sibling. One night when the dust had settled he had explained to her that their father had been such a transitory figure in their lives, even before their mother had died, that he had taken on the responsibility of Susan from childhood. It had explained a lot. Susan's adoration of her big brother and Taylor's indulgent humouring of his sister's sometimes excessive demands had fallen into place.

'I've missed you.' Susan placed a beringed hand on Marsha's arm once they were sitting in air-conditioned comfort. Mrs Temple—Susan's daily—bustled in a moment later with a tray of coffee.

Once the two women were alone again Susan leant forward, her light brown eyes—which were a washed-out version of Taylor's deep tawny orbs—uncharacteristically warm as she said, 'How are things, Marsha? What have you been doing with yourself?'

Marsha gave a brief description of her job and her home, to which Susan listened intently. Taylor's sister had never aspired to further education and she had left school at sixteen, working for a few hours a day in a flower shop before her marriage to Dale, when she had been just over twenty-one. At that point she had given up work entirely.

'And do you enjoy your job? Are you happy?'

There was something of an urgency to Susan's tone, which surprised Marsha. She looked at her sister-in-law, her smile soft at the other woman's concern as she said, 'Yes, I love my work. It's challenging and rewarding and every day is different.'

'But are you *happy*?'

Marsha took a sip of her coffee to give herself time to think. She had never worn her heart on her sleeve and she wasn't about to start now, but she couldn't in all honesty say she was happy, not even before Taylor had burst into her life again and turned everything upside down. She was satisfied with the life she had carved out for herself of necessity, and with that satisfaction had come more self-respect than she had ever had before, along with a belief in her own strength and fortitude, but happy? Happiness was Taylor. Joy was Taylor.

She took a steadying breath as she placed the delicate bone china cup on its fragile saucer. 'Happiness is different things to different people,' she prevaricated quietly, 'but can I tell you why I came today?'

'It's something to do with Taylor, isn't it?' It was more a statement than a question.

'He's told you he came to see me?' Marsha found she was faintly surprised. Susan and Taylor were very close, but somehow she had imagined he would keep the last few days quiet until they had sorted things out one way or the other.

Susan nodded, her eyes fixed on Marsha's face. 'He...he said you're still determined not to go back to him. Is that true?'

Again Marsha prevaricated. 'Susan, I just need to check a few things with you. Some of what he said—' She stopped abruptly. She really didn't know how to put this. 'He's adamant he never slept with Tanya or anyone else, not then and not since we've been separated. Could you have got it wrong?'

Susan continued to stare at her before bringing her lids down over her eyes as she reached for her own cup. 'You phoned the hotel yourself,' she said flatly.

'I know.' Marsha's stomach lurched. She had been banking on a ray of hope; she realised that now. 'Taylor said the booking was made in error—the double room for him and Tanya, I mean. He said he took the only other available bed in the place and shared a twin with another man at the conference. He maintains he wrote me a letter explaining everything—'

'Marsha, what do you want me to say?' Susan had set her cup down and now her face was tight as she raised her head again. 'You made the decision to leave him at the time and I don't see what's changed.'

Marsha returned her gaze for a long moment, then sank back against the sofa, putting a hand to her forehead. She had been clutching at straws; she saw that now. Susan was trying to be kind by not rubbing it in, but it was clear the other woman had no doubts about Taylor's infidelity. 'I...I want to believe him, I suppose,' she said throatily, tears welling up despite all her efforts to control herself.

'Oh, I'm sorry, Marsha, really.' Suddenly Susan was beside her, hugging her. 'But you've just told me what a great life you've made for yourself without him. You'll be all right. You will. You're so brainy and beautiful and...and nice.'

As her sister-in-law's voice broke and Susan began to cry with her, Marsha knew she had to get her equilibrium back. She should never have come here today. It could serve no useful purpose—simply opening the old wound until it was raw and bleeding.

She drew back a little from Susan with as much aplomb as she could muster, her voice still husky with tears as she said, 'It's me that's sorry, Sue. I've come here and upset you, and after all you did for me. It must have been hard, loving Taylor as you do, to tell me about Tanya and everything. Look, I ought to go.'

'No, no, don't.' Susan sounded almost desperate. 'Stay for a bit, please. Here, have some more coffee; you'll feel better.'

She couldn't feel any worse. Marsha dredged up a smile from somewhere as she nodded.

'I have missed you, Marsha, so much. I mean it.' Susan pushed back her hair from her damp face.

'Not with your busy social life, surely?' Marsha attempted to bring things back to normal, her voice brighter. Susan and Dale lived in a social whirl that would have made her giddy. She and Taylor had liked to go out quite often, dancing the night away at nightclubs, having and going to dinner parties or to the theatre, but they had also enjoyed quiet romantic dinners at home together, or weekends when they saw no one. Susan and Dale, on the other hand, rarely had an evening at home, and when they did it was usually because they were throwing a dinner party.

Susan shrugged now. 'Quantity of friends doesn't necessarily mean the quality is right,' she said, so bitterly that Marsha was shocked out of her own misery.

'Is anything wrong?' She placed a hand on Susan's arm.

'Lots. But then no one's life is perfect, is it?' Susan's smile was brittle now, and she made a show of pouring two more cups of coffee, removing herself back to her own seat as she did so.

The conversation was a little stilted from that point on, with Marsha telling Susan more about the TV company and the way things worked, and Susan responding by talking about the latest drama or film she'd seen.

It was as Marsha stood up to go that Taylor's sister reached out her hands again, taking Marsha's in her own as she said, 'You haven't told Taylor it was me? I mean, you haven't let anything slip that might give him an idea? He's so…'

As her voice faded away, Marsha acknowledged that she knew what Susan was trying to say. Her smile was crooked as she shook the other woman's hands gently. 'Of course I haven't. I gave you my word, but I wouldn't do that to you anyway,' she reassured her softly. 'We're friends, aren't we? More than friends—family.' For a little while longer, at least, until the divorce was finalised.

Susan's eyes flickered and then filled with tears, and for the umpteenth time since Marsha had come to the house the other woman surprised her by hugging her tight. Susan had never been physically demonstrative in all the time Marsha had known her, not even with Dale. The only person she had ever seen Susan hug of her own volition was Taylor, and even then it would be brief.

Marsha frowned over the other woman's head. There was definitely something wrong, and it was serious; she could sense it. She tried one last time. 'Sue, are you feeling all right? You don't seem yourself.'

Susan drew back immediately, brushing her face with the back of her hand. 'Thanks, but I'm fine,' she said, smiling now. 'It's just so nice to see you, that's all.'

She couldn't force a confidence if Susan didn't want to discuss it. Marsha smiled back, bringing a teasing note to her voice when she said, 'You just miss those shopping trips you used to drag me on, that's all.'

'We had fun, didn't we?' Susan said wistfully.

'Lots of it.' For the first time Marsha noticed that Susan's slimness bordered on the extreme. Taylor's sister had always been a fitness addict, spending hours at a local gym she belonged to, but now she appeared positively scrawny.

Marsha had phoned for a taxi some minutes earlier, and when the two women opened the front door it was just pulling up outside. 'Good timing.' Marsha smiled at her sister-in-law, determined to leave on a brighter note. 'It was good to see you again. Take care of yourself, won't you?'

Susan nodded. 'You too. I wish you would let me drive you back.'

'No need.' To be truthful, she needed to be by herself. 'And if I talk to Taylor I won't mention I called today. Okay?'

Susan nodded. 'Goodbye, Marsha.'

She had just sat down in the taxi and was leaning

forward to shut the door when Susan was at her elbow again. 'Could we meet occasionally?' she asked, with the urgency Marsha had noticed once or twice before. 'Have lunch, that sort of thing?'

Marsha didn't know what to say. This meeting had torn her heart out by its roots all over again, but it was clear that their relationship was important to Susan.

The only way she had been able to cope when she had first left Taylor was to cut herself off from her old life completely, and she was feeling like that once more. The pain was raw, but if Susan needed her…

She reached out her hand and took Susan's cool fingers in hers. 'In a little while, okay?' she said quietly. 'I need to make Taylor understand we can never get together again, that it is really over once and for all. Once the divorce is through I'll feel…easier about everything. But we will meet then, if that's what you want.'

She had tried to prevent it, but her eyes had filled up again as she spoke, and now Susan's face was distraught as she murmured, 'I shouldn't have asked.'

'Of course you should.' Marsha squeezed the other woman's hand one last time before settling back into the taxi. 'We're friends, and friends are always there for each other, whatever's happened.'

Susan shut the taxi door without saying anything more. As the vehicle drew away Marsha waved, but the other woman barely responded, although just as they turned the corner out of sight Taylor's sister was still standing at the bottom of the drive, staring after the car.

Marsha shut her eyes, letting out her breath in a deep sigh. So much for hope. She had been stupid to think Susan would say anything other than what she had eighteen months before. She didn't know why she had come now. As she'd told Nicki, Susan was Taylor's sister and she loved her brother devotedly. It must have been a real battle of divided loyalties for her.

She had to accept that it was really over, that there weren't any Prince Charmings left in the world who would ride in on their valiant steeds and rescue the fair maiden from whatever assailed her. Real life was different; *people* were different. People like her mother, her best friend. People like Taylor.

But she had thought he was special. It was the cry of a child in her heart. He had made her believe in happy ever after and that wasn't fair. None of this was fair. She had thought they would create their own family—not straight away, but in time. A family that would be a secure unit, strong, and who would do anything for each other. She didn't want to be alone the rest of her life.

No snivelling.

The voice in her head brought her up sharp, and she answered it by sitting up straight.

'All right, love?'

She became aware of the taxi driver's eyes on her in his mirror and she nodded quickly. 'Yes, thank you.'

'Only you look a bit under the weather, if you don't mind me saying so.'

'I'm fine.'

'Course, there's a lot of this flu about, you know. The wife went down with it a couple of weeks ago, and two of the kids are off school now. Mind, I reckon the little 'un is playing the wag. Don't like school, the little 'un.'

Marsha nodded, trying to be polite but wishing he would just drive the cab.

He must have got the message, because thankfully the rest of the journey progressed in silence.

She had rung Jeff at home first thing that morning, explaining that something unexpected had come up and she would like to take a day's holiday, if that was possible. 'Problems?' he had asked, and when she'd merely replied that they were personal ones he'd told her there was no need to use up any holiday time but, depending on how long it took to get things sorted, he would appreciate even an hour or two at the end of the day if she were able.

She found she was glad of this now. Her job was hectic and demanding, but that was exactly what she needed. The thought of going home to the empty bedsit filled her with dread. She would get to the office just before lunchtime and make sure she did not leave until she was too exhausted to do another minute. That way she might be able to sleep when she got home. Tomorrow was another day and she would think about everything then. For now it was enough to get through with her emotions so lacerated.

She had been an idiot when Taylor had called this morning. She had underestimated her own strength to resist him, but she wouldn't make the same mistake again. Her hands bunched together as she remembered their embraces, her cheeks flushing with humiliation at how easily he had beguiled her. From now on he could threaten to wake the whole street and she would not let him in. But it wouldn't come to that anyway. Tomorrow she would arrange to meet him somewhere anonymous, a wine bar or something similar, and she would make it abundantly clear the divorce was going through come hell or high water.

She caught her breath as her heart twisted. Behind

her closed eyelids she could picture him on the screen of her mind. His long lean tanned body as it had looked that morning, the broad muscled chest, flat stomach and hard powerful thighs, his hands—brown and long-fingered—and his mouth. Oh, his mouth… Sensuous, coaxing, possessing the power to send her delirious with desire. How was she going to manage without him? How would she ever get through the rest of her life, knowing he was in the world—walking, eating, breathing, loving—but not with her?

Stop it. She opened her eyes with a snap, furious at herself. She had got by the last eighteen months and she would do so again. Taylor Kane was not the be all and end all; she had to remember that. He might be fascinating and sexy and tender and magnetic, but he was also ruthless and arrogant and hard when it suited him. The same qualities that drew her to him drew other women, and she wasn't about to live her life ruled by jealousy, eaten up by it. This had to be a clean sharp cut which severed any fragile links still hanging between them.

She turned her head to gaze unseeing out of the window. Of course she would always love him, always carry a thousand regrets for what might have been, but she mustn't let him know that. She had thought she would grow old with him, loving him and being loved in return, but it wasn't to be. There would be no babies, no little Taylors with dark hair and tawny eyes…

Again she jerked herself out of her thoughts by sheer will-power. She must not let her mind stray for one moment. She had to keep absolute control over herself or she would end up a gibbering idiot! She had made the only decision she could eighteen months ago and nothing had changed. She couldn't spend her life wondering when he would tire of her completely, when one of his other women would capture his heart, mind and soul. Living alone for the rest of her life would be preferable to that.

The thought mocked her, especially because, having seen him again, she wasn't sure if it was true. If she thought there was a chance she might hold him she would take it.

But not at the cost of your own soul. She sat up straighter, her mouth setting in a grim line. And that was what it boiled down to. She wouldn't let herself become a victim, the sort of woman who put up with intolerable indignities in the name of love.

'Here we are, miss.'

As the taxi drew up outside the TV building Marsha scrambled out, giving the man a handsome tip to make up for being such an uncommunicative passenger.

She had made a life for herself and it was a good one. It *was*. It would have to be enough.

CHAPTER EIGHT

'MARSHA. I didn't expect you today.'

Nicki beamed at her as she walked into the office, which was a slight balm to her sore feelings. At least her secretary liked her, she thought with a heavy dose of self-pity which she wasn't about to apologise for in the slightest. 'I sorted things out quicker than I expected,' she said quietly.

'Sorted things out?' Nicki frowned. 'Jeff said you'd come back to work yesterday too quickly and weren't feeling great again today.'

Bless him. Marsha felt a brief warm glow in the leaden ball of her stomach. People could be so nice on occasion. 'Well, I'll stick to that officially, then. Unofficially—' she bent down closer '—I took your advice and went to see Taylor's sister.' She wasn't about to tell even Nicki of the early-morning breakfast scenario.

'And?'

'Nothing. She was very sweet and very upset, but that's all. The truth is the truth when all's said and done.'

'Pants.'

'Quite.'

Marsha seated herself at her desk and pulled a wad of papers in front of her. There was nothing more to be said.

When Nicki brought back half the canteen's stock of food at lunchtime Marsha ate a rather pitiable-looking ham sandwich and apple at her desk, but she had to force the food down. Jeff had popped his head out just after she had got into the office, declaring himself immensely pleased to see her, after which he had deposited a slim file in front of her, ordering her to stop all other work immediately. Marsha was not fooled by the width of the file. Thinking up ideas for new and interesting programmes was testing enough, but often necessitated a minimum of paperwork. Translating the idea into a programme within a budget, often with the impending broadcasting date just ahead, was the really hard work. After glancing through the paperwork she knew she would be working all over the weekend.

She had just returned to her desk, after a visit to the studio where the programme would be shot, and was immersed in a wad of possible facts and figures when Nicki leapt in front of her. 'Could you sign this please?' she said loudly, adding in a low hiss, 'Penelope and *him* are in the corridor outside.'

Marsha's stomach curled, but she had the presence of mind to keep her head down as she reached for the blank piece of paper Nicki had thrust on her desk.

Every nerve-end prickling, she waited for the door to open. She wasn't disappointed. Penelope sailed in first, in a cloud of cloying perfume, her tone pre-emptive as she said, 'He's in, I take it?' and made for Jeff's door.

'Just a moment, Miss Pelham.' Marsha was on her feet and in front of Jeff's door quicker than a dose of salts. She ignored the dark figure behind the other woman as she said, 'If you would like to take a seat, I'll just check Mr North is free.'

Penelope halted, swirling on her high heels as she said to Taylor, 'Really!' But she didn't press her case, knowing full well it was exactly how she would have expected her second in command to have acted.

Marsha knocked on Jeff's door, slipping inside and closing it again before she said evenly, 'Miss Pelham and Mr Kane are outside.'

'What?' Jeff had been deep in an intricate and soaring budget which had been giving him a headache for days, but as her words registered his eyes cleared. He disliked Penelope every bit as much as he liked Marsha, and he thought this Kane fellow needed his head testing. He didn't know what had gone on in the marriage—it might have been six of one and half a dozen of the other, though he doubted it—but for the guy to rub Marsha's nose in it with Penelope was downright cruel. And he had a pretty good idea what the 'personal business' Marsha had spoken about earlier involved. 'You okay?' he said softly.

Marsha put out her hand, turning it from side to side as she said, 'So, so,' her smile shaky.

'You know you're far too good for that bozo, don't you? Let Penelope get her claws into him for a while. He'll soon wish he'd never been born.'

Marsha's smile was more natural this time. 'Thanks, Jeff. I'll show them in, shall I?'

He nodded. 'And get Nicki to bring some coffee in, would you? Penelope takes hers with arsenic.'

'Oh, Jeff.' The kindness was a little too much, coming at a time when her composure was fragile to say the least. As the smile wobbled and her bottom lip trembled Jeff was round his desk in a shot.

'Hey, come on. No guy is worth your tears. Now, then—there's plenty out there who would give their right arm to be with you.'

He put a comforting arm round her shoulders, digging

in his pocket for a crisp white handkerchief with the other. He handed it to her with a wry smile. 'Chin up,' he said gently. 'Don't give either of them the satisfaction of seeing this bothers you.'

'I'll try.'

'That's my girl.'

'Oh, I'm sorry. Are we interrupting anything?' Penelope's cool voice from the doorway brought Marsha's blonde head and Jeff's brown one swinging round as though connected by the same cord.

Neither of them had heard the door open, but Penelope was standing staring at them, her eyes aglow, with Taylor filling the space behind her. Marsha gave an inward groan, but to give Jeff his due he maintained the stance for a second or so more, removing his arm from her shoulders almost leisurely as he said, 'We'll talk later, Marsha. Okay? Now, perhaps if you'd like to get Nicki organising that coffee...?'

'Certainly.' Taking her cue from Jeff, she raised her chin, speaking to the two in the doorway but keeping her eyes on Penelope's feline face as she said, 'If you'd like to take a seat?'

She let them come into the room before she made any effort to pass them, but even though she didn't glance at Taylor she could sense the dark waves emanating from the tall figure. Just as she shut the door she heard Penelope say in an overt whisper, 'Jeff, I'm so sorry. I had no idea. I thought Marsha was merely announcing us. If we've embarrassed you in any way...'

She might have known Penelope would turn the knife a little. Marsha took a deep pull of air as she stood outside the closed door, staring across the office.

'I couldn't stop her, Marsha.' Nicki was standing by her desk, her plump face agitated. 'She muttered something about she wasn't going to be kept waiting for anyone, and then just opened the door before I realised what she was doing.'

'Don't worry, Nicki, it wasn't your fault.' Marsha's voice was soothing, but she was working on automatic.

What on earth had it looked like in there to Taylor? She imagined their stance from his eyes. Nothing short of a clinch, that was what. Rats! She walked across to her desk, her tone preoccupied as she said, 'They want coffee, please, Nicki.'

As the other woman bustled off Marsha gazed down at the papers on her desk, but she wasn't seeing the figures in front of her. This was all she needed! Damn Penelope. It wouldn't make any difference that it was well-known Jeff was madly in love with his wife and a devoted family man; Penelope would have her last pound of flesh with this one.

She wrestled with what she could do or say until Nicki returned with the coffee, but once her secretary was seated at her desk again Marsha told herself she had to clear her mind and concentrate on the job in hand. She had very little time to organise everything, and all the agonising in the world couldn't turn back time. Taylor would have to think what he liked, and if any gossip started circulating Jeff was the sort of person who would nip it in the bud, Penelope or no Penelope.

It was only ten minutes later when the interjoining door opened, and although Marsha's stomach turned over she deliberately took her time about raising her eyes, keeping her expression calm and serene.

'I need to talk to you.' Taylor had stopped by her desk, Penelope by his side, and Marsha thought the other woman would burst a blood vessel when he turned his head, saying, 'I'll be along shortly, Penelope.'

'Fine, fine.' It was an immediate recovery, but Penelope was good at those.

Jeff, too, had paused, and now he said, 'We're going along to discuss a few items in this proposal with Tim. Can you cope here, Marsha?'

He was asking about more than the office and they were all aware of it. Marsha nodded, her voice steady as she said, 'Of course, but don't forget your appointment at four o'clock.'

'I won't.'

As Penelope and Jeff left Marsha turned to Nicki, who was all agog whilst pretending to work. 'I'm going to be here late tonight, Nicki. Could you pop down to the canteen and get something for my tea? A salad or sandwiches will do—something like that. I'll settle up with you when you come back.'

'Sure.' Nicki rose immediately, but not before she had given Taylor the once-over, her face unmistakably hostile.

It was Taylor who spoke first when they were alone. He perched on the edge of her desk, bringing well-cut trousers tight over hard male thighs as he said, 'She doesn't like me.'

'What?' It hadn't been what she'd expected.

'Your secretary. She doesn't like me.'

'Well, there has to be the odd female or two who are immune to your charms, surely?' Marsha said with a lightness she was proud of, considering the circumstances.

He eyed her steadily. 'Like to explain what that—' he indicated the office behind him with a jerk of his head '—was all about?'

A hundred sharp rejoinders burned on her tongue, but she didn't voice any of them. She stared at him for a moment or two, as though his words were taking time to filter through. 'I assume by ''that'' you mean the friendly arm round the shoulders?'

'Is that what it was?'

'Jeff is very happily married with two children. He is also a very nice man, who is a friend as well as my boss.'

Dark eyebrows rose. 'I've known several very happily married men who have the family-man image down to a fine art and also an obliging mistress on the side,' he said coolly.

'I don't doubt for a minute you are acquainted with that side of life,' she shot back tightly, 'but Jeff isn't.'

He shifted slightly and her senses went haywire. His suit jacket was open, revealing a crisp white shirt and a patterned navy tie, and as she watched he undid the first two or three buttons of the shirt, pulling his tie loose. It was a perfectly ordinary action and there was no call for the rush of sexual tension that sent electricity into each nerve and sinew.

'Penelope informs me you got this job on Jeff's recommendation.' He was still speaking in the conversational tone he had employed since he had left Jeff's office, but Marsha had lived with him too long not to know that he was the master of control and an expert in giving nothing away.

'I met him briefly when I was working for a different company before we were married,' she said, in a tone which stated that all this was none of his business. 'When I applied for the job here he recognised me. That's all.'

'And he made sure you got the position under him.'

There was a definite insinuation there, but she mentally shrugged off the insult. 'He believed in me, yes.'

'Penelope seems to think he does more than believe in you.'

'Really?' From somewhere was coming the strength to deal with this in a way she would have thought beyond her. 'Again, that doesn't surprise me. When one's morals are akin to a bitch in heat it must be difficult to recognise decent men and women.'

He leant forward, studying her with those clear orbs of amber light which were as penetrating as sunlight into a shadowed corner. 'So there is nothing going on between you and North?' he asked softly.

'No, there isn't.'

'Good.' He straightened, his arms crossed in front of him. 'I wouldn't have liked to have to make him see the error of his ways.'

Her head whipped upward. She just couldn't believe what a hypocrite he was. She glared at him, her voice frosty when she said, 'Have you got a replacement ready for Tanya yet?' her voice as double-edged as his had been moments before.

'Of course.' If he was aware of what she was implying he gave no sign of it. 'Tanya has been training her for three months now.'

'*Tanya* has?'

'Most adeptly.'

He smiled, and Marsha wanted to hit him over the head with her table lamp. 'Sheila Cross is fifty and re-entering the workplace after nursing her husband with terminal cancer for three years. She held a very impressive position with one of my competitors before her husband was taken ill, but when she became available for work again they implied she was too old. Their mistake, my gain. She might be a grandmother of two, but she's sharper than any twenty- or thirty-year-old. She'll keep the rest of the staff on their toes.'

Her eyebrows had risen at his unexpected elucidation. Ridiculous, *absolutely* ridiculous, in view of what she had had confirmed that morning by Susan, but she found she was immensely glad there wasn't going to be another sumptuous young thing pouting in front of him, with her notebook and pencil at the ready and her skirt up to her thighs.

She surveyed him now, her green eyes revealing more than she knew. 'Do you believe me, about Jeff?' she asked after a moment.

'Of course.'

He spoke so easily she knew it was true, and for some reason she found it annoyed her. Which was so crazy, so absolutely illogical, that she didn't understand herself at all. She didn't want him to be jealous, did she? she asked herself silently, and then was horrified with the answer.

'I'm sorry I had to shoot off this morning,' he said very quietly. 'I would have liked to stay and eat with you.'

Her cheeks began to burn in spite of herself. She tried to forget how magnificent he had looked and how good it had been, but it was hard with him so close.

'I phoned this morning, but they said you were unwell. When I called round at the bedsit Mrs Tate-Collins said you had gone out.'

There was an enquiry in his tone. Marsha felt her strength waver for a moment, then she told him the truth. 'I needed to go and see someone.'

'Someone?'

He was too close. She needed to distance herself a little or she would never be able to say what had to be said. If she could have chosen she would have picked a different place and a different time, but it hadn't worked out like that. She stood up, walking across to the window and then turning to face him again. He was watching her intently and he hadn't moved.

'I needed to go and see the person who told me about you and Tanya,' she said very clearly. 'I had to know if they could be wrong.'

'And?'

'They weren't.'

He remained perfectly still. 'I think I'm in a position to be the best judge of that.'

'They said—'

'*Who* said?' He stood up in one fluid angry movement, before controlling himself with visible effort. 'Who the hell is this person who seems to be able to convince you black is white? Damn it, I'm your *husband*. Your husband, Fuzz. My word ought to mean more than some nobody on the fringe of your life.'

'I'm sorry, but I believe them.' She met his fury steadily, knowing it would be fatal to weaken now. 'They have no reason to lie.'

'Then they are mistaken, if they aren't lying,' he ground out savagely. 'Either way they need straightening out.'

'Like you would have straightened Jeff out if we had been having an affair?'

'What does that mean?'

Her hand went to her throat, her fingers pulling at the flesh there before she forced herself to lower it to her side. He had often told her that one of the secrets of his success story was his ability to read the body language of his opponent. 'You bulldoze anyone who stands in your way—either that or you use your charm to manipulate and coerce them into submission,' she said flatly. 'But I won't allow you to do that here.'

'Charming.' He was furiously angry, more angry than she had ever seen him, and she was glad they weren't alone at her bedsit. 'You paint a great picture of me, sweetheart. I'll give you that.'

'You've told me often enough you came up the hard way.'

'The hard way, yes. Lying, cheating or double-crossing, no. I don't defraud or fleece some poor sucker who doesn't know what day of the week it is. Hell, if you thought I was like that why did you marry me in the first place?'

'Because I loved you.' She spoke without thinking, without realising that she was in effect confirming she had thought all those things of him. Which she hadn't—she really hadn't, she told herself in the next moment as she watched his face change into a man she didn't recognise.

'Well, now I know where I stand.' Instead of the previous white-hot fury, his voice and eyes were as cold as ice and without expression. 'Your opinion of me couldn't be much lower, could it? A shark, a twister, the sort of conman who is without conscience both in his personal life as well as his business enterprises.'

'I didn't mean that.' She had gone too far. She would have known that even if his whole being hadn't shouted it.

'That's exactly what you meant,' he said tersely. 'Damn it, I poured out my heart to you. I told you about all of my past and my dreams for the future. I didn't keep anything back. I thought if I told you how much I loved you you would begin to believe it. I wanted you to understand we had the kind of love that would last for ever, the kind that means intimacy and commitment and happy ever after. Everything you'd missed out on. Kids, grandchildren, growing old together. Laughing, crying and maybe even grieving, but always together. Always closer than our own skins. You were part of me, Fuzz. You were knitted into the marrow of my bones.'

Past tense. He was using the past tense. She stared at him, a sense of terrible finality gripping her.

'And all the time you had this secret opinion of me.'

'No—no, I didn't.'

He ignored her as though she hadn't spoken. 'I told you how it was with my mother and dad, how they made our lives a living hell. She married him because she was pregnant with me and immediately regretted it. Drink was the way she escaped from him and from reality and he knew it. Knew it and couldn't take it. She thought he was nothing and eventually he came to believe that himself. And do you know why? Because he loved her. If he hadn't loved her so much he would have fought back better, but she was all he ever wanted. Funny that, don't you think?'

He smiled, a terrible smile. 'Like father, like son? But I'm not going to go the same way as him, Fuzz. I'm not going to end my days wallowing in the gutter because the woman I love despises me. I'm worth better than that.'

'I don't despise you.' She was so shocked she could hardly speak, and even to her own ears her voice was feeble.

'That's not how it reads from where I'm standing.' His voice was low and harsh. 'You won't tell me who fed you that garbage in the first place, you give me no chance to defend myself—what's that if not contempt?

I married you knowing I couldn't wipe the first twenty-four-odd years from your psyche, but I thought what we had would survive anything that came against it. I was wrong.'

Struggling for calmness, Marsha said, 'Listen to me. You have to listen to me. I don't despise you. I've never despised you. I love you, Taylor.'

'Not enough.' His anger had collapsed, and in its place was grim intent. 'Not enough to trust me. Not even enough to phone that guy who gave me a bed. Did you think I'd bought him too? Forced and manipulated him like I apparently do with everyone else? Is that why you didn't pick up the phone *and call him*?'

'I told you, I didn't get your letter.'

'And so you were content just to cut your losses?'

'It wasn't like that.' If he knew the pain she'd suffered, the agony of wanting him so badly she'd been prepared to crawl on her hands and knees some cold lonely nights to find him…

'We had it and we lost it, and I still don't know the hell why.'

She flinched visibly, trying to think of something to say to take the dead look out of his eyes and failing utterly. She had blown it. Whatever happened now, she had blown it, and it was only in this moment of absolute truth that she could say in all honesty that she believed in him. Somehow, *somehow* there had been a mistake. Susan had listened to the wrong person, or maybe Tanya had lied, or perhaps someone else outside of the family had had something to do with all this. Whatever—he hadn't betrayed her. Only now there was no joy in the knowledge because she knew he would never have her back.

'I made love to you this morning.'

Every word was like a sword-thrust straight through her heart, but now she stood silent and still, knowing she deserved all this and more.

'Love, Marsha. We didn't have sex. We didn't mate like two animals who don't know any better. When I took you it was because I loved you—mind, body, soul and spirit. Every inch of you, the good and the bad, the weak and the strong. I would have died for you, don't you know that?'

'I…I believe you now,' she said with a desperation she made no attempt to hide. 'I do, Taylor.'

'No. Let's have truth between us if nothing else. You are convinced I slept with Tanya, and others besides, and this last little while it's Penelope I'm suppose to be bedding. Right? You married one hell of a stud, Fuzz. When did I get the time to sleep with all those women when we were still together anyway? Didn't you stop long enough to ask yourself that? You know how it was between us. We couldn't keep our hands off each other. Why would I have looked at anyone else?'

'I know, I know.'

The strains of a tuneless rendering of a popular chart hit from the corridor outside the office announced Nicki's imminent and tactful return, and now Taylor straightened, his voice deep and flat when he said, 'Goodbye, Marsha.'

What could she say to convince him to stay? How could they work this out? Coherent thought, let alone speech, seemed to be beyond her. She stared at him, watching as he opened the door just as Nicki returned. He brushed past the other woman without so much as a backward glance.

Nicki came in and shut the door behind her, depositing the goods from the canteen on Marsha's desk but saying nothing before she reached out her arms and hugged her. 'You'll be all right. You *will* get through this,' she murmured against her hair.

'I've made the worst mistake of my life, Nicki.' Strangely she had no desire to cry; the shock and pain were too deep for such relief. 'Somehow Susan was wrong.'

'Did you tell him it was her who told you?'

She stared blankly into the concerned face in front of her. 'I don't think it would have made any difference. He hates me, Nicki. I could see it in his eyes.'

'Oh, Marsha.'

They looked at each other and it was clear that for once Nicki didn't know what to say or do. Marsha glanced down at her hands, numbly noting how badly they were trembling. 'I must get on with some work.'

Nicki swore softly. 'Leave all that,' she said firmly. 'There are more important things at stake here than some old television programme.'

And this from a girl who lived and breathed her work. Marsha forced a smile, but it was a shaky one. 'You don't understand.' She shook her head, seating herself at the desk again as she added, 'How could you, when I don't understand myself? Somehow it's gone from bad to worse. All I know is it's too late, Nicki. Much too late. And at least I can handle this—' she indicated the papers littering her desk '—even if I make such a mess of everything else.'

'Maybe he'll come round?' Nicki was ever hopeful, that was one of the things Marsha liked about her, but today she knew her secretary was on a loser. 'Men do sometimes, when they've had a chance to think about things. My hubby often comes in with a bunch of flowers or a box of chocolates when he's been a pig.'

'But Taylor hasn't been a pig. I have.'

'Well, give *him* a bunch of flowers or a box of chocolates, then. Eat humble pie. It might not taste too good at the time, but it's very beneficial afterwards.'

'If it was as simple as that I'd do it like a shot, but it's not. He's given me loads of chances and I've blown every one.'

'But if he loves you?' Nicki argued. 'Try once more.'

Marsha shook her head. 'You don't know him,' she said quietly. 'When he makes up his mind about something he's like a solid force, immovable.'

Nicki sighed deeply, plumping herself down at her desk.

Poor Nicki. Marsha glanced at her secretary's woeful face. She so wanted this to end like one of the films or books she devoured so avidly, but this wasn't fiction.

She had lost Taylor.

CHAPTER NINE

MARSHA didn't leave the office until it was nearly dark. When she stepped outside the building the air was warm and moist, the smell of traffic fumes still heavy in the air although the rush hour was long since past. She stood for a moment flexing tired neck muscles. She felt utterly spent. And she would have to be back at her desk early in the morning both tomorrow and Sunday. So much for a relaxing weekend. But she didn't mind. She would rather be doing something than having time on her hands, the way she was feeling.

Tired as she was, she decided to walk home, and by the time she reached the bedsit it was quite dark. Once inside she kicked off her shoes, turning off the main light and clicking on a small lamp to the side of her TV. A shower. She nodded mentally to the thought. A long cool shower and then a cup of milky chocolate and bed.

The swirling in her stomach which had been with her since the confrontation with Taylor had prevented her from eating the salad and ham and egg flan Nicki had brought from the canteen, and when, after leaving the shower and pulling on her nightie, she felt light-headed, she knew she had to eat something. She forced down a couple of slices of toast along with the chocolate drink, and she was just finishing the last bite when the front door buzzer connected to her bedsit sounded.

Her heart jumped, and then raced like a mad thing. Taylor? Surely it could only be him at this time of night? She was shaking as she pressed the intercom, but her voice sounded quite normal when she said, 'Hello? Who is it?'

'Me—Taylor. Listen, Marsha, it's Susan. She's in hospital. She tried…' There was a pause before he continued, 'She tried to kill herself tonight.'

'What?'

'Dale found her. He's with her now, but she's upset and she's asking for you. Could you—?'

'I'll be down straight away.' She threw off the nightie, reaching for some clean underwear and pulling on a pair of jeans and a light top. She didn't even stop to brush her hair, grabbing her handbag and keys and racing down the stairs after she'd shut her front door.

When she opened the door to the building Taylor was standing waiting for her, his face drawn and grim. She wanted to fling her arms round him, but everything in his posture warned her not to. Whatever had gone on with Susan, it hadn't altered anything with regard to them, she realised.

The Aston Martin was double parked in front of the house, and as they walked towards it he said, 'I'm sorry about this. Did I wake you?' his voice horribly formal.

'No, I was late leaving work. I've only just got in and had something to eat.'

He nodded, opening the passenger door for her as they reached the car and then shutting it before walking round the bonnet. She watched him, her heart thudding. He looked ill, grey, but no wonder. Surely Susan couldn't have tried to take her own life? She had everything to live for.

As Taylor slid in beside her she said, 'There must be some sort of mistake, surely? Susan wouldn't have tried to kill herself.'

He started the engine, and it was only when he had pulled out of the cul-de-sac and into the main thoroughfare that he said flatly, 'Dale was going to Germany on some business for me this afternoon, but when he got to the airport he realised he'd left an important file he was working on at home at the house. He tried to ring Susan, but after a while thought she was either talking to someone for a hell of a time, or had taken the phone off the hook. Either way, he couldn't do without the file. He arranged to catch an early-morning flight tomorrow and called in somewhere for a meal and a cup of coffee before going home. He found her stretched out on their bed with an empty pill box beside her and half a bottle of whisky gone. She doesn't even normally drink whisky.'

'But why? Does he know why?'

'Apparently things haven't been right between them for a couple of years. They've been trying for kids more or less since they were married, with no results, and five years ago they started IVF, again with no results. Dale said Susan became obsessed by the idea of having a baby, it was all that mattered to her, so what does he do two years ago? He has an affair with his secretary.'

He made her jump by suddenly thumping the steering wheel so hard it must have hurt his hand. 'He maintains it was over as soon as it was started but Susan found out somehow. I could kill him, Marsha. If he hadn't looked like death warmed up tonight I swear I'd have strung him up then and there at the side of her bed.'

'Oh, Taylor.' She didn't know what to say. Why hadn't Susan told them? But then why should she? she answered herself in the next moment. It was none of their business what went on with Susan and Dale.

'She took it hard. He says he's been trying to make

it up to her ever since, but things have been bad. I guess the new house, the spending and the rest of it was all a consolation for having no kids, and she could just about get by with that, but when he had this affair she realised she'd got nothing.'

He was gripping the wheel so hard his knuckles shone white, his face dark with the rage he was trying to control.

'But she's going to be all right?' she asked faintly.

He nodded. 'But it was touch and go for a while. They've pumped her stomach, and she was out of it most of the time, but as soon as she came round enough to realise she hadn't succeeded in what she'd tried to do she kept asking for you. She wouldn't talk to Dale or me and she was getting hysterical, so I said I'd come and fetch you.'

'Did she leave a note, anything like that?' She couldn't believe this was actually happening. It was like a drama on TV, not something that happened to nice ordinary folk like Susan and Dale.

'I don't think Dale noticed anything, but then as soon as he saw her he realised what she'd done and panicked. He phoned the ambulance and then me, and dragged her downstairs, apparently, trying to make her walk and come to. I was at a dinner party in Sevenoaks, so I went straight to the hospital. I guess Dale will find out from Susan if she left a letter anywhere.'

Sevenoaks. Penelope had a penthouse pad in Sevenoaks. Marsha refused to dwell on the thought; there were more important things to hand. 'Do you know why she wants to speak to me?' she asked carefully. She had only seen Susan that morning after all. But she couldn't reveal that or Taylor would undoubtedly put two and two together.

He shrugged. 'She's barely lucid, poor kid.'

They drove in silence after that, and never had Marsha so bitterly regretted that they weren't still living together as man and wife. She desperately wanted to comfort him, to kiss the tautness of his mouth and tell him everything would be all right, but she had forfeited the right to do that for ever.

He had been absolutely right in all he had said since he had found her again. She *should* have stayed around long enough—when he had got home from Germany after that disastrous weekend—to dot the 'i's and cross the 't's if nothing else. And she should never have promised Susan that she wouldn't reveal who had told her about Tanya. She had accused Taylor of engaging in adultery and then refused to listen to any explanation because she had believed immediately he was guilty. Remorse rose like gall in her throat.

She hadn't believed in him and she hadn't trusted him. And why? He had hit the nail on the head the morning after he had taken her home when she had been ill. She had been waiting for him to let her down, like everyone else had in her life to date. She had never really given Taylor all of herself because she hadn't dared to, and the more she had come to love and rely on him, the more it had terrified her. She was a mess. A twenty-four carat mess.

By the time they drew into the grounds of the hospital Marsha felt less than the dust under his shoes. As Taylor helped her out of the car his touch was impersonal and his manner remote, the change in him heaping coals of fire on to her head.

She wanted to weep and wail and give way to the grief she was feeling, but now was not the time, and so she took refuge in the stoic reserve which had sustained her all through her difficult childhood and teenage years and beyond.

Once they had been admitted into the hospital she walked through the hushed, dimly lit corridors at Taylor's side with her head high and her heart breaking. She could cry for what might have been when she was alone, but for now she would conduct herself with dignity, if nothing else.

When they reached the small private room off a main ward where Susan had been taken, Taylor knocked once and opened the door, holding it for Marsha to walk through but not entering into the room himself. Dale was sitting by the side of the bed, and she saw immediately Taylor hadn't exaggerated how he looked, but all her sympathy was for the slight figure lying so still in the hospital bed. Susan's thin body barely made a mound under the cotton sheet covering her and she had her eyes shut, but as soon as Taylor spoke, saying, 'Has she said anything?' her eyes shot open.

As Dale shook his head, Susan said weakly, 'Marsha, oh, Marsha,' big teardrops beginning to trickle down her white face.

Marsha was aware of Dale standing to his feet and leaving the room, of the door being gently shut behind the two men, but as she took the too thin body in her arms, and Susan's sobs shook them both, her only thought was for the young woman who was her sister-in-law. She sat on the edge of the bed, rocking Susan gently as she murmured soothing words of comfort, and it was a long time before the storm of weeping faded to hiccuping sobs and finally to the odd gasp or two.

'Here.' Marsha reached for a big box of tissues on the bedside locker, lifting Susan's chin and mopping her face. 'That's better.'

As she smiled into the tragic face Susan surprised her by gripping her hand, her voice low and desperate as she said, 'Marsha, I've done an unforgivable thing. I left some letters before I—' She shook her head from side to side. 'Dale didn't see them, but he will when he goes home.'

'Susan, whatever it is, it can't be bad enough for you to do this,' Marsha said gently.

'It is.' Susan stared at her with puffy swollen eyes. 'I'm so ashamed. I wish they had let me die.' She turned her head to the side, fresh tears trickling down her face.

The bolt of lightning came from nowhere, causing Marsha's whole body to become still. She moistened her lips with her tongue before she said, 'You made it up—about Tanya.'

Susan's body jerked. 'You knew?' she whispered.

'Not until this moment.'

'He...he never did anything, not with Tanya or anyone else.'

Susan was gripping her so hard she would have bruises, but the pain didn't register. As she stared into Taylor's sister's eyes, Marsha had a strange feeling come over her. For a moment she almost felt as though she was suffocating, and it was an enormous effort to say, 'Why did you do it?'

'I don't know, not really. I think I was a little deranged at the time, but that's no excuse, I know that. Dale...Dale had an affair with his secretary—'

'I know. He told Taylor tonight,' Marsha cut in.

'He did?' Susan wiped the back of her hand across her face but still held on tightly to Marsha with the other one. 'It made me feel...like nothing. Less than nothing. I couldn't have a baby and now my husband had been with someone else, *slept* with her. There was only

Taylor in my life who loved me, that's how I felt, but now he had you I wasn't really important to him like I used to be. Everything had changed.'

'Susan, Taylor's always loved you. You're his sister. His own flesh and blood.'

'But you would give him babies, children and grandchildren, and I would get more and more pushed out.'

'That would never have happened.' Marsha stared into the other woman's eyes, the pale orbs filled with misery and looking far too large for the elfin face.

'I know that now, I knew it soon after you had left Taylor, but it was too late by then. I couldn't say what I had done. He used to come and see me and rage against the person who had told you such lies, say what he'd do to them when he found out who it was. He will never forgive me, Marsha. He'll hate me now.'

Marsha looked at her, torn between pity and anger and pain and regret and a hundred other emotions besides. Struggling to put her own feelings aside for the moment, she said, 'Taylor could never hate you, Susan.'

'He could for this. From the moment he met you he worshipped the ground you walked on, and even before I knew you I was so jealous of you. But then… Well, you were so nice, and we got on so well.' Susan swallowed. 'And then I found out about Dale. I…I felt it must be my fault that he had wanted someone else. I wasn't good enough or pretty enough. I went on medication from the doctor but it didn't seem to help. I couldn't sleep, couldn't eat. I used to get up in the middle of the night when Dale was asleep and walk round the neighbourhood, wondering why all the other women in all the other houses could keep their men and I couldn't.'

Marsha reached out her hand and stroked a lock of

damp hair from out of Susan's eyes. 'Why didn't you tell someone?' she said softly. 'If not me, then Taylor.'

'Taylor would have beaten Dale to a pulp, and then there was Dale's job. It would have become impossible for him to continue working for Taylor and then where would we have been? But the main reason was…' Susan lowered her eyes, her voice becoming nothing more than the faintest whisper. 'I felt so humiliated, so ashamed—about Dale wanting someone else, the fact I couldn't have a baby, everything. I…I didn't feel a woman, Marsha, just a thing. An ugly, fat, barren thing.'

That was why Susan had become fanatical about working out at the gym and dieting, Marsha thought, not long after she and Taylor had married. 'You should have told me,' she said gently.

'I've never been good at sharing my feelings at the best of times,' Susan admitted pitifully. 'With Mum like she was there was no time for anything like talking or discussing any troubles. I can never remember her hugging or kissing me in the whole of my life. And of course Dad was never around, and on the rare occasion he was he was too busy fighting with Mum to take any notice of me or Taylor.'

'Oh, Susan.' Marsha's eyes were dry but she was crying inside. For the small bewildered and hurting child trapped in Susan's body, for Dale, who clearly hadn't got a clue how to handle the emotional volcano he had married, for Taylor, for herself. Susan's jealousy had led Taylor's sister down a lonely twisted path to a place where the outcome had been devastating for everyone.

'I've told Taylor everything in the letter I've left.' Susan was clutching at her again, her whole being begging for absolution. 'And there's one for you and one for Dale too. I've explained about your letter, the one that Taylor wrote you just after you had moved out and were living in that bed and breakfast.'

'You took it?'

'He told me what he was going to do, and so the morning after he'd posted it I said to Dale I was going jogging early. I hung about across the road from where you were staying and when I saw the postman I jogged over to him and pretended that I lived there. I asked if there was anything for a Mrs Kane and he handed me the letter. It was as simple as that.' Susan rubbed at her damp face. 'It's amazing how if you're deceitful enough you can fool nice people, isn't it?'

'And you made the reservation in Germany.' It was a statement, not a question, but Susan answered it anyway.

'I knew the hotel, because Taylor uses the same one every year when he goes to the conference, so it was just a matter of phoning and changing the two single rooms Tanya had booked for one double. They didn't even ask for an e-mail or anything to confirm.'

'And so you waited until they'd gone to Germany and then came and told me.' Marsha stared at the girl she had thought of as the sister she had never had.

Susan nodded, her voice husky from the effects of the treatment she had had as she said, 'I can't believe I did all that now, I really can't, but it was strange. One thing led to another and it was like I was on some kind of a high, like I was proving I wasn't so stupid and worthless somehow. When I got the letter that day I went to the gym in the afternoon and worked out for hours I had so much adrenalin.'

'Have you still got the letter?' Marsha asked numbly.

Susan shook her head. 'I was worried Dale might find

it. He has thought it's been the affair that has been between us for the last year or two, that I would never forgive him, but it wasn't that. How could I tell him what I'd done to you and Taylor? He would have despised me.'

'Do you still love him?' Marsha asked quietly. She couldn't sort out her own feelings, they were too confused and raw, but the fact that Susan had tried to take her own life and was clearly ill was at the forefront of her mind.

What Susan had done once she could do again, and although a therapist might be able to help her in the long term, she needed forgiveness right now more than anything. It wouldn't help anyone to rant and rave.

'Yes, I love him.' The words were softly spoken through trembling lips. 'And I can see why he had the affair. I pushed him away with the baby thing. I got so that having a child was all-important and I forgot I had a husband with needs of his own. The way it's been since I split you and Taylor up I've expected Dale to walk many times. He's certainly had good reason to, but he hasn't. He has been blaming himself for the affair; I've been blaming myself for what I've done to you and Taylor…'

Her voice trailed away and she shook her head. 'Can you ever forgive me, do you think? I know you won't straight away, but do you think you can in time?'

'I forgive you now.' How could she do anything else with that skeletal body and those agonised eyes in front of her? Whatever Susan had done, she had paid a high price the last eighteen months. Marsha reached forward, hugging Susan again as she reiterated, 'I mean it, Sue. I forgive you, okay? But you must promise me you'll get help.'

The thin body stiffened for a moment, and then Susan relaxed against her. 'A psychiatrist? Someone like that, you mean?' she whispered.

'Whatever it takes. If you talk to the doctors here they will be able to guide you to the right person, I'm sure. Do you promise me you'll do that?'

'I promise. And everything will be all right between you and Taylor now, won't it? Now you know the truth? You can be like you were before,' Susan pleaded, her voice muffled against the silk of Marsha's hair.

Susan was still such a child at heart. Marsha was glad Taylor's sister couldn't see her face at that moment, and she cleared her countenance of all expression as she drew away.

Susan thought all she had to do to put things right for them was to confess, and then the last eighteen months would be wiped away. But it wasn't as easy as that. Irreparable damage had been done—something Taylor had made clear today. In fact it really did not matter now who had told the lies about Tanya; they had gone past that. She hadn't given Taylor even a tiny measure of trust or commitment of the heart, and he knew it. If he had been with Penelope tonight, who could blame him?

Susan was still staring at her, so now she forced a smile, saying, 'Things will work out, Sue, but for now just concentrate on getting well, okay? Look, I'm going to go now, but I think you ought to tell Dale and Taylor yourself.'

'Not Taylor.' Susan clutched at her again, her grip surprisingly strong for one so frail. 'I could tell Dale, but I just couldn't look at Taylor's face, I couldn't.'

'I think you owe him that.'

'I'll tell Dale first,' Susan said after a moment or two.

'And then perhaps he will stay with me and we'll tell Taylor together?'

Marsha nodded, rising from the bed as she said, 'I'll send Dale in, shall I?'

'Yes, please.'

When Marsha turned and looked at her sister-in-law again before opening the door, Susan's fingers were working at the bedcover like a very old woman. She was ill, there was no doubt about it, Marsha thought as she smiled a goodbye, and she did feel sorry for her, but it was hard to believe that someone she had thought she knew could set out to be so horribly destructive.

Taylor and Dale were sitting in the small waiting room a stone's throw away, and as Marsha walked in she felt you could have cut the atmosphere with a knife. It was clear Taylor had spoken his mind about a few things, and when she told Dale that Susan wanted to see him he couldn't get out of his chair quickly enough.

'Do you mind if I sit down a moment?' Marsha said quietly.

There was a cold light in Taylor's eyes as he looked at her, waving his hand for her to take the seat his brother-in-law had vacated, but just at that moment Marsha felt if she didn't sit down she would fall down. She knew it hadn't really sunk in yet—Susan actually attempting to end her life besides her amazing confession—but the strange calmness and self-control which had been with her while she'd spoken with her sister-in-law was slipping away. It had probably been born of shock, she acknowledged, but at least it had helped her not to say anything she would regret later.

'How is she?' Taylor's voice was no warmer than his eyes.

'Calmer.'

'Would you like a cup of coffee?'

They were talking as though they were practically strangers and it hurt. 'No, thanks. I must be getting home in a minute.'

'I'll take you.'

As Taylor made to rise to his feet Marsha said hastily, 'No, it's all right, really. Susan said she wanted to speak to you in a little while and you ought to be here. I can get a cab.'

'As you wish.'

He really didn't care one way or the other, Marsha thought, the jagged edge of pain banishing the last of the anaesthetising calmness. He had cut his losses and moved on mentally. What would he feel when Susan admitted she was the instigator of the gigantic tangle their lives had become? He would forgive his sister, the hardest heart couldn't hold out against the pathetic creature Susan had become, but would he feel her loyalty to her sister-in-law was laudatory or otherwise? She really didn't know.

'Taylor? Earlier, at the office, I never meant to imply you would cheat or defraud someone. I've never thought that.' She had to take this one last chance to try and make him see how sorry she was. 'I was mixed up and terribly off beam about everything, I know, but—'

He interrupted her quietly but grimly. 'Excuse me if I'm wrong, but what's adultery if not the ultimate cheating?'

She stared at him, desperately trying to find words to explain how she felt. He had accused her of not loving him enough, but the truth of the matter was that she loved him too much. 'I meant what I said this afternoon, about believing you,' she said at last. She hoped he would remember she had believed him before Susan had told her what she'd done.

He raked his hair back, his jaw tense. 'Marsha, let's not do this, okay?'

'But you have to listen to me.'

'Why? Why do I have to listen to you?' He banged his fist on the coffee table in front of him as he spoke, making her jump a mile. His eyes blazing, he bit out, 'You've never listened to me. Not when you first found out about this supposed affair and not since. How do you think I could have made love to you if I had touched someone else? How do you think I could have done that? And this morning, after what we had shared, you still didn't believe me. You preferred to take the word of someone else and you wouldn't even give me their name.'

'There were good reasons for that.'

He went on as if she had not spoken. 'I don't believe you didn't receive my letter, Marsha. Whether you ripped it up unread, I don't know. That's more than possible, the state you were in, I suppose, and it would explain why you didn't ring the number I'd given you. Or maybe, like I said earlier, you thought I'd bought myself out of trouble by paying the guy to lie for me? Whatever—it's history now, and I'm sick to death with it all.'

With her. Sick to death with her, he meant. White as a sheet, Marsha stood to her feet. 'I had better go.'

Through clenched teeth he said, 'Yes, I think you'd better.'

Let me not fall at his feet and beg and plead with him to love me again. Let me walk out of here and out of his life with some semblance of dignity.

She had reached the door and begun to open it when he said, 'Marsha?'

'Yes?' She kept hold of the door as she turned her head.

'Thank you for coming to see Susan tonight.'

She inclined her head in acknowledgement before stepping out into the corridor and shutting the door carefully behind her. His voice had been flat, all the hot anger gone, and somehow it convinced her more than anything else that had gone before that he really had washed his hands of her.

When she climbed into the black cab and a cheery voice said, 'Well, hello there. It's you again. Remember me, love?' Marsha almost groaned out loud.

Instead she tried to look pleasant when she said, 'Yes I remember.'

'I picked you up this morning.'

'Yes, I remember.'

'You don't look any less peaky, if you don't mind me saying so.'

She did mind, she minded a lot, but it wasn't this poor man's fault her world had fallen into pieces around her. 'I've got a headache.'

'Oh, yes? The wife has headaches. Blimey, does she have headaches. Sick with it and everything.'

'Really?' Please shut up. Please, please shut up.

'Mind, she has them sometimes for convenience an' all. Know what I mean?' He chuckled to himself, apparently oblivious to the lack of response in the back. 'But she's a good woman and I wouldn't change her. Six kids we've got. You got any kids?'

'No, I haven't.'

'Married?'

Just. 'Sort of.' She didn't know why she added, 'I'm getting a divorce soon, actually.'

'Oh, yes?' He shook his head. 'You look too young to have to go through that, and he must be a silly so-an'-so to let a nice girl like you go.'

Marsha found herself provoked into saying, 'The divorce is my fault, actually.'

'Is that so?' There was silence for a moment. 'But you don't want it?'

She was startled into looking up and meeting the eyes in the mirror again. 'Who says?'

'Me.' She could tell he was grinning. 'You learn a lot about human nature when you drive a cab.'

She said nothing to this, hoping he would take the hint.

He did. Right up until she got out to pay the fare. 'Thanks, love.' She hadn't given such a generous tip this time, but he didn't seem to mind. 'And, look, if you don't want that divorce, you tell him, right? You march up to him and tell him straight. Things can't be worse than they are now, can they? So what have you got to lose apart from a little pride? And pride makes a cold bedfellow.'

Marsha found herself smiling with genuine warmth. 'Thank you,' she said quietly.

'You going to take my advice?'

'I might.'

'The next time I pick you up I shall ask, mind.' He chuckled again, before revving the engine and disappearing in a cloud of exhaust fumes.

CHAPTER TEN

WHEN Marsha let herself into the bedsit she didn't bother to put on the main light, preferring the muted glow from the lamp at the side of the TV, which she had left on while she was out. She walked over to the sofa, sitting down and remaining in the same position for long minutes in a kind of stupor.

Eventually she glanced at her watch. One o'clock in the morning. She had to get to bed. But she still didn't move. She felt exhausted, both mentally and physically, but she knew she wouldn't be able to sleep.

When the telephone rang five minutes later the one name in her head was Taylor, so it was with crucifying disappointment that she heard Jeff say, 'Marsha? Is that you?'

She rallied enough to say, 'Who else would it be at one o'clock in the morning?' in a fairly normal voice, continuing, 'What on earth are you ringing for at this time?'

'I'm sorry to wake you—' he didn't sound sorry, more excited '—but we've had one hell of a breakthrough with regard to the Baxter story. There's an old boy who used to work for Manning Dale, their chief accountant, and he's prepared to spill a few very tasty beans. Seems Baxter was a friend of his at one time and he's just found out about his death. One of our researchers made contact with him purely by a fluke, but it looks like it'll pay dividends. The problem is...' Jeff paused for breath '...the window of opportunity is extremely narrow. This guy, Oswald Wilmore, is going to see his son in Australia for six months and they'll be travelling round the Outback and so on. If we don't nail a few facts now we can forget it.'

'When does he leave?'

'The flight departs Heathrow in twelve hours' time. Now, as this has been your baby all along, I wondered if you wanted to go and see him. Otherwise I shall leave in the next ten minutes. The researcher's with him as we speak. Apparently they've been sharing a bottle of whisky,' he added drily.

'Where does this Oswald live?' Marsha asked weakly. What a night! And to think earlier she'd thought the most arduous thing she'd be doing this evening was drinking a mug of milky chocolate before going to bed!

'The near side of Watford. Do you want to do it?'

Penelope's beautiful feline face floated in front of her eyes. 'You bet,' she said, with more enthusiasm than she had ever thought she'd feel again after the last caustic hour with Taylor.

Jeff spent another five minutes filling her in with a list of dos and don'ts, and then she found herself flying round the bedsit, collecting everything she would need after phoning for a taxi.

Fifteen minutes later she was sitting in a cab on her way to Watford, all exhaustion burnt up in the flood of adrenalin coursing through her body. Oswald had apparently agreed to say what he had to say on camera, so a small crew were meeting her at the old man's house, along with one of the presenters. If Oswald really was prepared to dish the dirt on Manning Dale it would be a tremendous scoop. Marsha thought briefly of

Baxter's widow, a gentle woman with sad eyes, and hoped Oswald wouldn't chicken out at the last minute.

He didn't. Apparently he had been with Manning Dale from its beginnings, the founder having been a personal friend. Some years before he had retired, and after his friend had died, the man's sons, who were now in charge, began sailing very close to the wind. By then Manning Dale had become a corporation, formed by the merging of separate and diverse firms and—in Oswald's own words—a monster intent only on satisfying its lust for more and more power. Ethics, codes of practice, morality, personal conscience had all become dirty words to those at the reins.

'You nail the blighters—all right, love?' Oswald said in an aside to Marsha whilst the others were loading equipment back into the van. 'My old friend would be turning in his grave to think his lads had done the dirty on Charles Baxter. And don't forget, if you need me to come back and say anything more I'm willing. What's your second name, by the way, in case I need to talk to you while I'm gone?'

'Marsha Kane.' It was out before she thought about it, probably because Taylor had been there at the back of her mind all the time, and she hastily added, 'But my working name is Gosling. Marsha Gosling.'

'Kane?' The elderly man nodded. 'Unusual name. I don't suppose you're any relation to Taylor Kane of Kane International?'

Marsha stared at him. 'He's my husband,' she said faintly.

'Is that so? Well, I watched your husband build up his business from when he was a young whippersnapper. Success stories like that get talked about in business, you know, and I admired him. Oh, yes, I admired him all right. If my friend's sons had been like Kane we wouldn't be having this conversation right now. A hard man, mind, but fair with it. No skeletons in the cupboard there. But of course you'd know that better than most, eh?' He smiled at her, quite unaware he was turning the knife in the wound of her burning guilt.

'Thank you, Mr Wilmore, but we really have to be going now.' She had backed away from him as though he was the devil, rather than an upright seventy-year-old pillar of the establishment.

'Oswald, dear. Call me Oswald.'

Marsha was having a lift back to the TV offices with the presenter, who had come up in her own little red convertible. Bobbie was a bubbly redhead with inch-long eyelashes and a very firm idea of where her career was going and how to get there. She oozed confidence, along with plenty of sex appeal, if the cameramen were anything to go by, and was witty, bright and articulate. Marsha felt like someone's aged grandmother in comparison.

This was the sort of woman Taylor should have married, she told herself during the eternity of listening to Bobbie's conquests near and far on the journey back. The presenter would never imagine for a single moment that the man in her life was going to leave her, neither would she be crippled by self-doubt and diffidence. The world was Bobbie's oyster, and because she always expected a pearl to be lurking under the shell it invariably was.

Oh, Taylor, Taylor. Now the urgency of the interview was over the pain and self-recrimination she had been keeping at bay by working flooded in, along with the exhaustion twenty-four hours without sleep had induced.

Bobbie, on the other hand, seemed to get more animated and buoyant the nearer to base they got. On at least two occasions Marsha seriously considered jumping out of the car when they stopped at traffic lights, Bobbie's chatter having reached a pitch which had become unbearable. Only the thought of how much pleasure Penelope would get from such a story stopped her.

But then, at last, the building was there in front of them, and when Bobbie suggested she drop her off before she went and parked Marsha didn't argue.

It being a Saturday morning, Marsha knew Nicki and quite a few others wouldn't be in. Jeff, however, had been planning to come in and work on the material he had given her yesterday, so she intended to drop off the notes she'd gathered and brief Jeff on Oswald before going home to bed.

As she walked into her office Jeff's door opened and her boss's head peered round the aperture. 'Come on in here. I've got the coffeemaker from home going,' he said jovially, all smiles. As well he might be. The programme was going to be a winner. They'd all known it before Oswald, but now top viewing figures were a dead cert, Marsha thought as she followed him into the much larger room.

'You look rough,' was Jeff's opening remark.

'Thanks very much,' she said tartly. 'Considering I've been on the go for twenty-four hours and missed umpteen meals, I think I look pretty good.' She hadn't looked in a mirror for hours, but she wasn't about to tell him that. Neither was she going to confide that it wasn't lack of sleep or food that was the problem, but a six-foot-something man with eyes the colour of dark honey.

'Sit down.' He pushed her down into the big leather

chair opposite his own, the desk between them, and poured a cup of coffee from the machine perched on a little table next to him. It tasted wonderful.

'What's this?' He had placed a large brown bag in front of her, and when she opened it she found four rounds of bacon sandwiches.

Jeff produced a bag of his own as he said, 'Present from the wife. She reckoned you might be a bit peckish by the time you got back here.'

'How nice of her.' Marsha was really touched.

'She thinks I work you too hard.'

'She's right.'

'Fill me in on what you've got, and then we'll have another cup of coffee and eat.'

'See what I mean?' Marsha said ruefully.

'Slave is in your job description. Now, shoot.'

When she had finished telling him everything Jeff lay back in his chair and laughed out loud. 'We've got 'em tied up tighter than the hangman's noose. I'd like to see Penelope's face when you tell her what you've got.' He pushed the bag towards her. 'Now, eat up or the missus will think you don't like her food.'

They were on their second cup of coffee, Marsha's shoes having been discarded so she could flex her aching toes and an inch-thick bacon butty in her hand, when footsteps outside followed by a sharp knock at Jeff's door brought her straightening in her chair. The next moment Taylor was standing in the doorway. He was wearing the same dinner suit he'd had on at the hospital, now crumpled and creased, his five o'clock shadow had passed midnight and his hair was rumpled and most un-Taylorish. Marsha thought he'd never looked so handsome.

'I've been looking for you,' he said to her, after the

briefest of nods to a surprised Jeff. 'You weren't at the bedsit, and Mrs Tate-Collins didn't know where you had gone.'

'There was a rush job. Jeff phoned me last night when I got in from the hospital.' She couldn't move, couldn't think, and even to her own ears her voice was flat.

'Susan told me everything.'

He obviously expected her to make some response, but the numbness was holding. She felt weird, cold and shivery, frozen to the core of her being. She dared not hope that his being here meant anything. Her hopes and fears had had such a see-saw of a ride the last few days before finally being shattered beyond repair.

The silence between them stretched until it was painful, vibrating with tension as their eyes held, and it was Jeff who eventually couldn't stand a second more. 'Marsha's been in Watford since the early hours,' he said much too loudly, in an effort to be normal. 'The wife's provided bacon sandwiches all round and there's plenty. Care for one?'

For a moment she thought Taylor wasn't going to reply, but as she finally managed to wrench her gaze from his he turned to Jeff, his voice still very quiet when he said, 'Thank you. I'd like that.'

'Here.' When Taylor still continued to remain exactly where he was, just inside the room, Jeff stood up, moving one of the spare guest chairs from the far wall beside Marsha. 'Sit down, won't you? How do you like your coffee?'

Taylor seated himself, his eyes on Marsha again. 'Black, please,' he said absently.

Although she had her eyes centred on the mug in her hand, Marsha was aware of every inch of the long lean body next to her. She was horrified to find she was trembling, and drank half a mug of coffee scalding hot in an effort to still the shivering within.

After Jeff had placed a mug of coffee and a bacon sandwich in front of Taylor, he said, 'I've just got to pop out for a minute. Too much coffee. You know how it is…'

Neither of them acknowledged his going, but he hadn't expected them to.

'I didn't know where you had gone,' Taylor said softly when they were alone.

'I had to go on a rush job,' she repeated, her voice little more than a whisper.

'You can't have had much sleep.'

'No.' She found she couldn't raise her eyes to his. 'I haven't had any.' There was another pause, and then she said, 'How's Susan?'

'She was asleep when I left. Dale is going to stay with her and bring her home once the doctor has been later today.'

'So she'll be all right?'

'Eventually. They think she had a kind of breakdown round about the time she told you—' He stopped abruptly, shaking his head before he continued, 'Anyway, she needs help, that's for sure. She weighs next to nothing, and Dale told the doctors she roams about the house most nights because she can't sleep. He's been trying to get her to see a doctor for months. Having said all that, I have to admit if it was anyone but Susan I'd say she's got exactly what she deserves for what's happened to us.'

'But it is Susan,' Marsha said gently, meeting his eyes.

He stared at her, his gaze moving over each feature

of her face. 'You really don't bear her any ill will, do you?' he said, a touch of wonder in his voice. 'She said you'd forgiven her, but I thought it might be just because you didn't want to upset her last night.'

'Of course I've forgiven her.' For you, if nothing else.

'Thank you. Look, do you want that?' He gestured to the sandwich hanging limply in her hand.

She shook her head. She had thought she was hungry when she'd walked into Jeff's office, but now the whirling of her stomach made eating impossible.

'How soon can you leave here? We have to talk. You know that, don't you?'

She swallowed hard. He hadn't given her any ray of hope that he had softened regarding her treatment of him, but nothing on earth would have stopped her leaving with him. 'I've already told Jeff all he needs to know.' She placed her mug on the table. 'We can leave right now, if you like.'

He nodded. 'I do like.'

'I'll just write a note explaining that we had to go and I'll see him Monday morning.'

She found her hands were shaking as she scribbled a quick message, and she was vitally aware of Taylor on the perimeter of her vision. The ruffled hair and crumpled clothes were so at odds with his usual immaculate appearance it was disturbing, mainly because he obviously hadn't taken the time to go home and shower and change before he came to find her. But that didn't necessarily mean anything, she warned herself in the next moment as her heart leapt and raced. But, against all her efforts to stifle it, hope had risen again.

Her heart continued to thud alarmingly as they left the office and travelled downwards in the lift to

Reception, and it was after she had smiled and waved a goodbye to Bob that a thought struck her. 'How come Bob let you through without ringing my office first?'

Taylor reached in his pocket and produced one of the slim security passes all the employees were issued with. 'Kane International is supplying and installing that new equipment, remember? Penelope thought it would be a good idea if I could pop in at any time.'

Marsha just bet she did. Hope fizzled and spluttered and died again.

The Aston Martin was parked in one of the top executives' slots in the car park, which was so like Taylor that Marsha would have smiled if she'd been able. Taylor opened the passenger door and she slid inside, grateful to be sitting down again because she really was feeling most peculiar.

'You're worn out.' As Taylor joined her in the car the tawny gaze moved over her face.

Well, at least he hadn't said she looked rough, as Jeff had, even though it was obviously what he was thinking. She nodded, turning to glance at him and then finding her eyes held by his. The hard, handsome face was grim, his gaze holding her own with a searching intensity as he spoke. 'There's no excuse for the things I said to you.'

'What?' It was the very last thing in the world she had expected him to say.

'I should have known you wouldn't take the word of just anyone about Tanya, that there had to be something vital in the fact you wouldn't reveal a name. And the letter...'

'No, I can see why you wouldn't believe I hadn't received it,' she said quickly. 'The chances of it being lost or something were so small. It's me that's done everything wrong. I didn't trust you when I should have—'

'How could you?' He interrupted her bitterly. 'Susan orchestrated everything, down to the last nut and bolt, and she knew how vulnerable you were—knew your background. She played on your fear of being rejected, hitting all the right buttons. I still find it hard to believe my little sister was capable of such cruelty.'

'She wasn't in her right mind,' Marsha said softly, hating to see the pain etched in the rugged features and knowing the torment he was going through.

'She was sound enough to ring the hotel and change the booking before she told you, and also to intercept that letter.' His voice broke and he raked back his hair with a savage movement which spoke of his inner frustration and anger.

'Taylor, you have to remember it wasn't the real Susan at that time,' Marsha said, working through her own resentment at what his sister had done even as she spoke. 'The real person, the one you know and love, is the woman who has been racked with guilt ever since. She told me how she felt when she found out about Dale's affair—worthless, less than nothing, not even a woman. She couldn't have babies and now Dale didn't love her like she'd thought he did. That's how she was feeling. And...'

She took a deep breath, knowing she was going to probe a painful wound. 'And if I had trusted you, like I should have, none of what she did would have succeeded. But believe me on one thing, please. It wasn't that I didn't love you enough; it was that I loved you too much. It frightened me to know you were my world, my everything. I just couldn't believe someone like you would want someone like me for the rest of our lives.'

'Oh, my love.' He moved in his seat, leaning over her and taking her mouth as he pulled her hard against him. It wasn't a gentle kiss, it was one born of need and frustration and pain, but it was a lover's kiss, long and deep and hungry, and it left her physically and mentally shaken to the core.

'You're my everything—you know that, don't you?' he murmured against her lips as the kiss ended. 'I've been in hell since you left, crazy half the time, angry, tortured by thoughts of you with someone else. I just couldn't believe you wouldn't come back to me, that you wouldn't work out for yourself how much I loved you, that I could never betray you.'

'I'm sorry. I'm sorry.' His words were like little burning darts in her heart. She had hurt him so much. How could he still want her?

'No.' He put a hand to her lips and she was touched beyond measure to see it was shaking. 'It was me that was wrong. I should have known you were still too damaged by what had happened in your past to have confidence in yourself as a woman. We hadn't had enough time together before the attack came. Maybe if it had happened five or ten years down the road, when we'd had children and our family unit was strong, it might have been different. As it was, I expected too much.'

'It was your right to expect I should trust you,' she said, her tears like tiny diamonds as they hung on her lashes.

'Maybe.' He gathered her to him again. 'But what has right got to do with anything? I should have understood better, loving you like I do. It was only when we got so close to the divorce that I realised you really weren't going to come back. Then I panicked.'

'You did?' She stared at him, eyes wide and still glittering with tears. She couldn't imagine Taylor panicking about anything.

'Oh, yes.' He touched her mouth gently with the tip of a finger. 'I knew I couldn't live the rest of my life without you, so I had to do something—swallow my foolish pride, get off my butt and make you see the truth. I knew you loved me—' he managed to sound both magnificently arrogant and uncharacteristically humble '—but that clearly wasn't going to be enough to persuade you to come back. When I heard about the possibility of tenders for equipment at the company where you worked it was perfect. I could hassle you at work and at play. Of course I hadn't reckoned on the formidable Penelope.'

She couldn't believe she was in his arms, so close she could feel the thud of his heart with the tips of her fingers where they rested against his shirt. 'She likes you.' She looked into his eyes, remembering the painful jealousy she had felt. 'She had you lined up as her next conquest.'

'I'd sooner mate with a praying mantis.' Penelope was dismissed and put out of the way as their lips fused again, seeking each other greedily before at last Taylor lifted his head reluctantly. 'Any more and I'll take you right here in full view of the world,' he said huskily. 'Are you coming home?'

Home. The word sang in the quintessence of her mind, provoking such emotion that she could only nod her answer.

As the engine roared into life she found she was tingling with anticipation, her skin alive from the tips of her toes to the crown of her head, even as her brain still grappled with the fact that her misery was over.

Neither of them spoke on the way back to the house. All the threads could be unravelled later. For now it was enough that they were together again.

As the car pulled up on the drive the front door opened immediately, Hannah's bulk nearly filling the doorway. Marsha saw the housekeeper's eyes widen at the sight of her, but she merely met her on the steps, putting her arms round her in a bear hug which took her breath away as she said to Taylor, 'Dale phoned a few minutes ago. The doctor has been and said Susan can leave, so he's taking her home. He explained a little of what's gone on.'

'We'll talk later.' As they stepped into the hall Taylor patted Hannah's arm. 'Okay? For the moment we're going to sleep. Marsha hasn't slept in over twenty-four hours, and I only had cat naps at the hospital. If anyone phones, tell them I'm in bed with my wife and can't be disturbed.'

Hannah beamed.

They climbed the stairs hand in hand, but when Taylor opened the door to their bedroom and they walked into the beautiful room Marsha felt suddenly shy. Hannah had opened the windows, and the perfume from the lavender bushes was warm in the air, the huge bed with its soft billowy covers dominating the room as always. For a moment she felt like a bride again, and it was a strange feeling.

'Shower or bath?'

'What?'

Taylor smiled, reaching for her unresisting body and bringing her into the haven of his arms. 'Shower or bath before we turn in?'

She thought of the massive corner bath where they had loved so many times before. 'Bath.'

He left her to start the bath running, returning almost immediately to where she was still standing, slightly dazed by the swiftness with which everything had changed. She was home, home with Taylor, and the nightmare was over.

She didn't have time to think anything more. He covered her lips with his in a kiss of such hunger that all lucid thought fled and she gave herself up to pure sensation. She melted against him, sliding her hands over the rippling muscles in his back as she pulled him even closer. They fitted together so well, curves dissolving into hard angular male planes like a perfect jigsaw. How could she have stayed away so long?

'I've dreamt of this for eighteen months,' he murmured hoarsely. 'Eighteen months of cold showers.'

'There was the other morning,' she protested faintly, the words more of a sigh.

'That's not like having you here, where you belong. I want to undress you, touch and taste you, tease you. I want to wake up beside you and know I only have to reach out my hand and you are there, soft and silky at the side of me. I want…' His mouth kissed the tiny pulse racing wildly at the base of her throat. 'I want everything.'

He undressed her slowly, kissing every inch of her skin as he did so, peeling her clothes from her with an enjoyment he made no effort to hide. She gasped as the slightly callused pads of his fingers stroked across her engorged breasts, the peaks hard and aching, and then smoothed down over her flat stomach to her thighs.

His tongue left its teasing of her lips and his mouth began an exploration of where his fingers had touched, and now she pulled at his clothes, anxious to have nothing between them. When his clothes had joined hers, her breath caught in her throat at the beauty of him—tall, wide-shouldered and lean-hipped, strong and totally male.

'Come on, wench.' He caught her up in his arms, carrying her into the bathroom, where he laid her gently in the silky warm foaming water. She raised her arms to his, bereft at the loss of the feel of him, and he laughed softly, joining her in the bath a moment later.

'Let me wash you.' He gathered some foam in his hands, running them over her shoulders and down her arms before he turned his attention to her breasts. His fingers traced an erotic path around her nipples, becoming tantalisingly slower until they reached the very tips.

'Think of all the baths together we've missed,' he whispered, before ducking his head to take possession of one taut peak. 'We'll have to stay in here for a month to make up for lost time.'

Taylor wasn't satisfied until he had washed every inch of her, stroking and caressing until the sexual tension in her body grew unbearable and she felt she would explode if he touched one more inch.

'How about you?' She swished backwards in the water, reaching for a bar of soap on the side of the bath. 'I'm not sure if you're clean enough to share my bed.'

'Scrub away.' He grinned at her, spreading his arms along the side of the massive circular bath as she moved towards him. She knelt over him in the water, lathering the soap between the palms of her hands before beginning to gently massage the tanned clear skin of his throat and neck, moving to the broad expanse of his muscled chest when she was done. She curled the rough smattering of body hair on his chest round her fingers, teasing and caressing before she stroked the small nipples.

It felt wonderful to be with him, and the last eighteen months faded into a bad dream as she grew accustomed to every muscle and contour of his body once again. The warm water, the hard male body and the ripples of pleasure causing each nerve-end to glow seemed like a dream, a dream she never wanted to wake up from.

When her hands moved down to his flat stomach she felt him tense, and she didn't prolong the agony, stroking and cradling his manhood as she murmured, 'I think this needs special attention.'

'And how.'

The next moment he had pulled her to her feet, his breathing ragged as he said, 'Let's go to bed.'

In spite of the fact that they were both exhausted their union was no quick, lusty coming together, but a long, slow reacquaintance with every inch of each other's bodies. The almost desperate urgency which had gripped Taylor at the bedsit was gone. Marsha was home and they had all the time in the world.

They touched and savoured, their hands and lips almost reverent as the enormity of what they had come through dawned afresh in the wonder of being together in their bed once more. They whispered words of love, promises that never again would they doubt each other or be apart.

Marsha felt drugged with pleasure as Taylor tasted and teased and nibbled the silky smooth skin of her throat, her breasts, her stomach, her body aching for a release only he could give. It was an enchanting journey back into their world, their secret world, where no one else could intrude.

When at last Taylor eased himself between her thighs she was moist and ready for him, accepting his swollen fullness with a little moan of pleasure. Even then

Taylor's control held for long minutes, until eventually the time was right. They both shattered together, going over the edge into a world of colour and light and sensation.

It was some minutes before either of them stirred, locked together in each other's arms as they were. Marsha raised her hand, touching Taylor's face as she traced a path over his chin.

'I should have shaved.' He opened his eyes and smiled ruefully.

'Later.' She snuggled into him, waves of tiredness washing over her like a warm tide. 'Everything can come later.'

And they slept.

Neither of them heard the telephone ring, or Hannah's voice informing Penelope, as per Taylor's instructions, that Mr Kane was in bed with his wife and couldn't be disturbed.

EPILOGUE

IT WAS June again, the sun blazing down out of a clear blue sky and the scent of lavender heavy in the air. Marsha adjusted her position in the big easy chair under the shade of an umbrella, smiling to herself as she watched Taylor and Dale splashing about in the pool with Susan and Dale's twin girls.

Who would have thought five years could make such a difference? she thought idly, glancing at Susan, fast asleep at the side of her. No one had been more surprised than Susan and Dale when, six months after Marsha and Taylor had got back together again, Susan had discovered she was pregnant.

The birth of the twins had transformed Susan. She had ceased seeing her therapist, throwing herself into motherhood with gusto and enjoying every minute of it, hectic though it had been at first. Night feeds, screaming babies, lack of sleep—nothing had got her down, and Dale, Taylor and Marsha had looked on amazed as the thin, sickly creature of the past had turned into a plump matron who took everything in her stride.

'I don't know who enjoys playing more. The twins or Dale and Taylor.'

Susan's voice at the side of her brought Marsha's head turning again, and she saw her sister-in-law was awake.

'Definitely Dale and Taylor.' She giggled, watching

as they each tossed a little screaming infant into the air before catching them again before they hit the water. 'I think—' She stopped abruptly, shutting her eyes and breathing fast for a few moments. When she opened them again Susan was starting at her anxiously. 'That was a strong one,' Marsha said calmly.

'You're having pains?' Susan sat up so quickly her lounger rocked. 'Why didn't you say? How long have they been coming?'

'An hour or two,' Marsha said serenely, rubbing her huge stomach as the pain left her. 'Don't worry. Most people aren't like you.' Susan had given birth to the twins within two hours from start to finish, nearly giving Dale a heart attack when they'd got stuck in traffic a mile from the hospital. He had practically collapsed with relief when they finally reached it, the first baby being born just ten minutes later. 'First babies take ages.'

'I'm telling Taylor.'

Taylor was out of the pool like a shot, and at her side in seconds. 'How strong are they? Have your waters broken? Are you timing them?'

Marsha looked at him fondly. He had come to every antenatal class, and she appreciated that, but he had been like a cat on a hot tin roof the last few days since she had gone past her due date.

'I'm fine,' she said gently. 'There's ages to go yet. We'll be able to have the barbecue as planned.'

Taylor said something very rude about the barbecue, and Dale, who had now joined them, with a little arm-banded figure on each hip, added, 'Susan was saying there was ages to go ten minutes before ours were born.'

'Only because we were stuck in traffic and I didn't want you to panic.'

'I'm taking you in.'

When Taylor spoke in that voice Marsha knew she had no option, so, grumbling loudly, she lumbered to her feet, plodding into the house but having to stop halfway when another pain hit.

She sat in the hall with everyone fussing over her, and Hannah scurrying about like a chicken with its head cut off collecting her hospital case and things, and within moments—or so it seemed—Taylor was back downstairs, changed and ready.

He looks flustered, Marsha thought in absolute amazement. She had never thought to see her cool, contained husband in a spin, but she was seeing it now.

'How many contractions since I've been upstairs?'

'One—and did you know you've got one black and one brown sock on?'

'Damn my socks. How far apart in minutes?'

'Five.'

'Five?'

'I think the beginning of the pains must have been the backache I've had the last twenty-four hours,' Marsha supplied helpfully. 'It sort of worked its way round into the front a couple of hours ago, and— Oooh…' This time the contraction was strong, very strong, and once it had died down Taylor gathered her up in his arms, despite her vehement protests, and carried her out to the car, his face white under its tan.

'It's okay.' When he joined her in the car, after stowing her case in the boot, Marsha put a comforting hand on his. 'Women have babies every day, you know.'

'You are my wife, and this is my baby, and it doesn't happen every day to me.'

'Shouldn't that be our baby?' she asked drily. 'And from where I'm standing it's happening to me, not you.'

'You know what I mean.'

She did, and she loved him for his concern. She would probably never see Taylor in full panic mode again—unless it was with subsequent babies—so she settled back to enjoy every moment of it.

When they arrived at the hospital Marsha hadn't had a pain in the last ten minutes, and when she told Taylor this, once he had parked and was helping her out of the car, he groaned loudly. 'Don't do this to me.' He put a hand on her stomach, patting it gently. 'Do you hear me in there? Your old dad can't take any false starts.'

'I don't think this is a false start, Taylor,' Marsha said, looking down at her feet. 'My waters have just broken.'

By the time she was lying in bed in one of the delivery rooms the pains were back to every five minutes, and Marsha was reflecting that Taylor was probably the only father who had managed to be presented with a cup of tea to steady his nerves before the event. In fact the two midwives who were dealing with the five mothers who had all decided to give birth at the same time seemed far more interested in Taylor than they did her.

All that changed as time went on. Three of the mothers had given birth to bouncing baby boys, the midwife who had taken over Marsha's confinement announced, and Mrs Dodds next door was due to produce any moment. It looked like Mrs Kane was going to be the last, didn't it?

Mrs Kane didn't care if she was the last or the first, as long as this baby got a move on, and Mr Kane echoed that sentiment with every fibre of his being. He wouldn't have believed someone as fragile-looking as Marsha could have the grip of a sumo wrestler, but he seriously wondered if she had broken his fingers—again.

Samuel Taylor Kane was born at five in the evening, and he made it a fivefold whammy for the male sex that day, according to the smiling midwife. When Marsha looked into the tiny screwed-up face, above which was a ridiculously thick mop of black hair, she fell immediately and hopelessly in love. As did his father.

Taylor sat on the edge of the bed with them, gazing in rapt wonder at the nine-pound bruiser who was his son, tears on his cheeks. 'I love you,' he said softly to Marsha, touching the baby's silky hair with a gentle finger. 'So much.'

'I love you too.'

'No regrets about giving up work?'

She smiled at him. The Baxter story had been the sort of scoop which had ensured she got noticed by the powers-that-be, and when she had been promoted to controller, with a very tasty salary increase, no one had been surprised. She had enjoyed the last few years, but when she and Taylor had started trying for a baby she had known she wanted to be at home with it full time. She needed to give this baby, and the ones to follow, all that she had never had. 'Not one.' She could always take up her career again later if she wanted to. For now being a wife and mother was supreme.

'Thank you for our son.'

'You did play a part in the proceedings.'

'Only the easy bit.' He grinned at her, looking more gorgeous than he had any right to when it was going to be another six weeks at least before they could make love.

'That's true.' She brushed the tears from her own face, wondering why it was you cried when you were more happy than you'd ever been in your life. 'We're a family, darling.'

'That we are,' he whispered, sliding an arm round her and pulling his wife and child into the shelter of his body. 'That we are.'

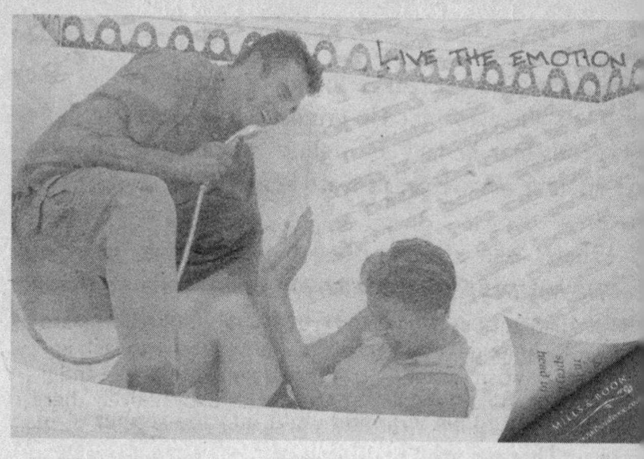
LIVE THE EMOTION

0804/01b

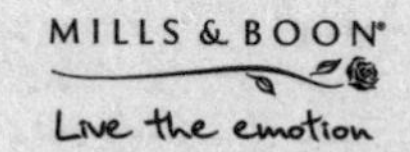

Modern romance™

LUCA'S SECRETARY BRIDE *by Kim Lawrence*

Luca O'Hagan is supposed to be meeting his brother for dinner – instead he finds himself alone with his brother's beautiful secretary! The attraction he feels for Alice can't be ignored, and he has to have her. But Alice is a woman with secrets, and Luca discovers he can never have all of her…

THE MILLIONAIRE'S LOVE-CHILD *by Elizabeth Power*

Annie Talbot discovers her son was accidentally swapped at birth, and then that her powerful and sexy ex-boss Brant Cadman has her child and she his! Annie knows she and Brant have a sexual chemistry that cannot be ignored – because they once had a one-night stand…

THE AUSTRALIAN'S MARRIAGE DEMAND
by Melanie Milburne

Jasmine didn't expect to wake up beside best man Connor Harrowsmith the morning after her sister's wedding! She's made a genuine mistake, but as she leaves his room the paparazzi of Sydney are waiting. Connor insists they wed, but is he thinking of more than a marriage on paper…?

THE UNEXPECTED PREGNANCY *by Catherine George*

Harriet Verney crosses paths with billionaire James Edward Devereux when she sells him her home. His presence makes Harriet's pulse race faster – especially when she wakes to find James at the end of her bed. Soon there is nothing standing in the way of their attraction – or of Harriet conceiving their child!

On sale 3rd September 2004

Available at most branches of WHSmith, Tesco, Martins, Borders, Eason, Sainsbury's and all good paperback bookshops.